To our good fri[...]

Life is a mystery.
Enjoy yours.
Al Eden

The Mystery
of the
Phantom Ship

Al Eden

authorHOUSE®

AuthorHouse™
1663 Liberty Drive
Bloomington, IN 47403
www.authorhouse.com
Phone: 1 (800) 839-8640

This is a work of fiction. All of the characters, names, incidents,
organizations, and dialogue in this novel are either the products
of the author's imagination or are used fictitiously.

Published by AuthorHouse 06/14/2019

ISBN: 978-1-7283-1557-7 (sc)
ISBN: 978-1-7283-1556-0 (e)

This book is dedicated to the loving memory of my uncle Rob, my aunt Ann, and my mother Jean. If you are wondering…. YES, they all saw the Phantom Ship.

Acknowledgement

I would like to thank my daughter Ashley. She inspired and encouraged me to publish this book. She spent many long hours editing and re-editing. Without her, this book would not be as good as it is.

CONTENTS

FOREWORD

The inspiration of this story is based on Al's childhood vacations at his uncle Rob's farm in Shigawake, Quebec. The story is loosely based on these visits with a lot of mystery and imagination, and a large serving of fantasy thrown in. The characters in the story are based on Al's aunt and uncle, mother, older brother, and himself. He also felt the story needed a curious and loveable little girl, named Molly. He is happy to share his story with others, so they too can experience the mystery and imagination that he encountered as a child.

The Legend

Many long years ago in Shigawake, a little fishing village south of the Gaspe Peninsula, a pirate ship continually attacked and robbed fishing trawlers and pleasure crafts. The remains of these boats often drifted back to the shore with no signs of the survivors or their treasures. Countless searches turned up nothing and the pirate ship was never seen, except by those poor souls who disappeared into the darkness and depths of the Chaleur Bay never to return.

It has been thought and recounted that late one spring night, after looting and pillaging another craft, the pirates were celebrating and drinking when a scuffle broke out, knocking over a lantern and setting fire to a barrel of rum. Soon the pirate ship was ablaze and a wall of flames turned the night sky into day. Horrific screams from burning pirates filled the air as they jumped to their deaths into the frigid waters of Chaleur Bay. The following morning all that could be found was the charred remains of the crow's nest and a small section of the ship's mast. Still to this day, the remains of the ship have not been recovered.

Many years later, the fishermen and sailing enthusiasts began to feel a sense of security and peace, while sailing the once again shimmering waters of Chaleur Bay. This was until a recurring and mysterious illusion continued to haunt the inhabitants of this small fishing village. This was the illusion of the Phantom Ship.

Locals have said that late at night, during the spring and fall, a glowing ball of light rises up from the stillness of the bay and then takes the fiery form of a three-masted sailing ship. It has been said, that the Phantom Ship, engulfed in a wall of flames shoots fireballs that die out as they hit the water. This is accompanied by the ghastly screams and eerie sounds that fill the cool night air.

Many fishermen and boat enthusiasts have gone to investigate this strange phenomenon, after witnessing it themselves, to find nothing, while friends on shore watch as they sail right through the place where the Phantom Ship had last been seen ablaze. For those who have witnessed this strange phenomenon, they have found the Phantom Ship to be disturbing to the point where it becomes engrained in their memories forever. It may seem like some sort of illusion, but it is unsettling, disturbing and more than just an illusion.

So begins my story...

CHAPTER 1

The Secret

Gord, Adam, and Molly, were visiting Uncle Rob's farm during their Easter vacation with their mother Jeanie. The children always loved to visit the farm and looked forward to their new adventures each year. Uncle Rob's farm was about 300 acres. He had 40 milking cows and also raised cattle for beef. He grew oats, barley, potatoes and other vegetables. He raised pigs and chickens too. This made him a very busy, and hard-working man, which was seen by those closest to him. Uncle Rob was an older, weathered man with rough hands, tanned skin, and despite the pain he felt from the demands, he always had a smile on his face.

Molly was eight years old and was a handful. She was very bright, always busy, and seemed to be a trouble magnet. She was always happy and loved to talk to anyone who would listen. Her long brown curly hair cascaded from every direction and her freckled face was usually covered with dirt. She often was found wearing a plain t-shirt and jean overalls. Dresses were pulled out only for special occasions, upon Mom's request.

Adam was ten years old. He looked intelligent with his black horn rimmed glasses and perfectly parted dark brown hair. He was always neat and tidy with his shirt tucked into his pants. He spent most of his free time reading and he had to know how and why everything worked. Adam always sought out an explanation for everything and this often sparked a debate with his older brother.

Gord was the oldest, at thirteen. He was a happy go lucky boy and nothing seemed to faze him. He was tall, lean and lanky, and a little uncoordinated because he was growing so fast. This however, did not prevent him from exploring.

After a day of exploring and visiting the animals, helping with a couple of the chores, and enjoying a marshmallow roast by the bonfire, the kids were in their rooms getting ready for bed.

Molly overheard Uncle Rob talking to Tim, the hired hand who had been down on the beach collecting driftwood. Tim enjoyed whittling the driftwood into souvenir sail boats which he sold to craft shops in town. Tim was recounting the strange occurrence of the sighting which he referred to as "The Phantom Ship," and seemed strangely quiet. Molly crept halfway down the staircase to where she could hear and see the men talking. She made sure to stay out of sight. Uncle Rob had a troubled look on his face. For just last year he had told Tim that he had also seen the Phantom Ship when he was down at the beach fishing grunion. The flaming lights and the eerie screams were still fresh in his memory.

A shiver came over Uncle Rob and he said, "I don't know where or what the heck that Phantom Ship is, but it just gives me the creeps every time someone talks about it."

Molly crept quietly upstairs without being seen. She was fascinated, confused and just a little scared. She couldn't wait to tell Gord and Adam about what she heard, but seeing that it was just before midnight she rolled over, hugged her stuffy, and fell asleep.

In the morning Molly was awakened by a soft gentle breeze that made the lace curtains dance at the foot of her bed. She jumped from her bed barely taking time to smell the scent of the cherry blossoms that grew up to her window. She ran downstairs to the playroom where the boys were sleeping.

"Gord, Adam, wake up!" she bellowed.

"There better be a good reason for you to wake us up," said Gord sleepily.

"I overheard Uncle Rob and Tim talking about some strange ship. They called it the Phantom Ship."

"Did they say anything else about this weird ship?" asked Adam

"They were talking about some eerie screams and a burning ship. It all sounded quite creepy to me," exclaimed Molly. "They both seemed to be very spooked as they discussed what they had seen," she continued.

"Wow, that was worth waking us up for," said Gord. "Sounds like this should be investigated." Adam agreed, but decided they needed to make a plan.

When the kids came up for breakfast, Uncle Rob was already in the barn doing the morning milking. Aunt Ann and their mom, Jean were drinking coffee and talking about making cookies for the church bazaar. Aunt Ann, a Roly-Poly lady with a round face to match her big round belly, always had a smile on her face and a hug for whoever ventured near. She was a sweet lady that loved to bake, and the kids really enjoyed this.

"Come and sit down," Aunt Ann said. "I made you sausages and pancakes with maple syrup."

"Aunt Ann, tell us about the Phantom Ship," said Molly. Aunt Ann turned a sombre shade of white as a blank expression enveloped her face. There was a long pause and when the colour finally returned, all she said was, "Eat your breakfast." Something was definitely suspicious, but Molly knew that they were not going to get any information from Aunt Ann. The rest of the meal was unusually quiet, as each of the children wondered why Aunt Ann was so scared of this mystery.

After breakfast Adam and Gord went out to the barn to help Uncle Rob with the chores. The boys were collecting eggs and helping with the milking, all the while, thinking about the morning they were having. Adam looked over at Uncle Rob while he sprayed some milk for the barn cats, and asked "Uncle Rob, can you tell us what you know about the Phantom Ship?" There was a long pause and he cautiously replied, "I don't know what you are talking about."

With a puzzled look on his face Gord replied, "But Molly heard you and Tim talking about it last night." Uncle Rob, beginning to feel uneasy and, as a worried look crept across his face, replied "Well Molly must have been dreaming, I know nothing about the Phantom Ship." Gord was not sure what to think. He knew that Molly had a vivid imagination and maybe, just maybe, her imagination was running wild; after all, she had stuffed her face with roasted marshmallows, s'mores and hot chocolate the evening before. "I wonder why everyone is so hesitant to talk about the Phantom Ship," Gord said to Adam.

Maybe Tim would share some information, after all

he was a simple man. Adam and Gord went over to the blacksmith shed where Tim was repairing a horse shoe for the big Strawberry Roan. Uncle Rob used this horse to pull the plough for planting crops because he was so strong.

"Tim, tell us about the Phantom Ship," asked Adam. The same eerie silence and ghostly stare that the boys had just seen on Uncle Rob's face, and on Aunt Ann's face was now occupying Tim's as well. Tim, clearly flustered, snapped at the boys and angrily snarled, "Don't bother me, can't you see I'm busy!"

Now Adam was sure that something was wrong and asked Gord "Why won't anyone talk about the Phantom Ship?"

"I don't know," said Gord, "But we have to find out."

Gord and Adam decided that later that night they would investigate this strange occurrence that no one on the farm, would talk about.

CHAPTER 2

The Plan is in Place

The boys waited for what seemed like forever, until they were quite sure that everyone in the house was sound asleep. Gord and Adam quietly crawled out the basement window and onto the dew covered grass. This was enough to wake Molly and she rushed to the window.

"Wait for me," she called out to the boys. Gord, annoyed by the curiosity of his little sister said, "Go back to bed, you are too little to come."

"I will tell Mom if you don't let me come," she whispered.

"O.K." said Adam, "Just be careful." Molly put on her favorite red sweater and slipped out of the window, then carefully climbed down the cherry tree.

The three musketeers stole quietly down the dirt road to the gate, which was covered in course gravel. Just across the road, was a thick and dark hay field that had a well beaten path that led to the edge of the beach. This was a path that had clearly been travelled many times before. The full moon lit up the nighttime sky and cast a shimmering light on the calm ripples that danced towards the shore. Adam had anticipated problems and had brought a flash light, a blanket, some nylon rope, matches, a candle, and his trusty pocket knife. Gord also made sure to bring along a bag of Aunt Ann's cinnamon buns and a bottle of juice.

Upon arriving to the beach, the children were careful as they scaled down the side of the large rocks that littered the edge of the beach. All was quiet except for the sounds of the water lapping against the shoreline and a faraway haunting cry of a loon.

Without warning, the moon dropped behind a dark cloud and cast a disturbing light above it and to the right. Suddenly a deluge of rain started to fall and the three children ran to the shelter of the over hanging rocks. Gord leaned against a large flat rock which gave way and fell backwards with a thump. It was hiding the entrance to a shallow cave.

"We are in luck," said Adam. "We can stay dry until the storm subsides." The kids stepped across the rock and huddled together under the blanket for what seemed like a long time. Adam shone his flashlight around the cave; nothing appeared unusual until the light glanced over a tiny opening in the east wall. There was a cold draft of air coming from the opening. It sent shivers up Molly's spine and she cried, "I want to go home!"

"We can't go home now," exclaimed Adam, "We have to find the Phantom Ship." Slowly and hesitantly, the children crawled along the opening as it was not big enough to stand up. After a few short minutes the tunnel grew wider and emptied into a dark cavern. Molly looked around and said "This cave looks about the same size as my bedroom. I wouldn't want to sleep here though!"

At the far end of the cave was a hole about three feet around. A strange bright light reflected on the rain soaked walls near the hole. As the children ventured closer to investigate, they could hear blood curdling screams off in the distance.

"Let's go back," Molly begged.

"No," Adam said, "We have to find out if that is the Phantom Ship." Even though Adam's neatly parted hair was standing on end and there was a disturbing chill running down the back of his neck. He had to know where the mysterious light and screams were coming from.

"Maybe the bright light on the wall WAS the Phantom Ship," exclaimed Gord.

"I don't care what that was, I just want to go home", Molly sobbed. "Can we PLEEEASE go home?"

"Let's just go a little bit further and see if there are any clues as to what that light was, or where those noises were coming from," reasoned Adam. Molly grabbed Gord's hand and whispered "Please keep me safe, I am scared."

As they crawled further through the cave the rain had subsided and so had the noise. Molly sighed with relief as she saw another entrance to the cave, just up ahead. When the children left the cave they looked out on the Bay. The moon had come out from behind the clouds and the water was once again calm. The only sound that could be heard was the water lapping against the rocks. The three children were extremely quiet. They kept looking out over the bay, but saw nothing. The sand was wet and cold beneath their feet. Gord looked down at his watch and realized how late it was getting. "We'd better get back to the farm," he said to his siblings.

It seemed like a much longer walk back to Uncle Rob's house than it had been going there, now that the kids were tired and cold. Gord, Adam, and Molly were damp and just a little bit scared and confused. They crept back into the house and crawled into their beds without being noticed. All of the children had a hard time falling asleep that night, as the eerie screams and the light on the wall, took over their thoughts.

When they awoke the next morning around 10 o'clock, Aunt Ann said "You sleepy heads sure were tired. Uncle Rob must have worked you hard yesterday." No one said a word but they all exchanged knowing glances. Finally Gord spoke up and said, "It must be the fresh country air, Aunt Ann."

Molly, Gord, and Adam helped Uncle Rob split and stack firewood early that afternoon, yet the whole time they couldn't help but to think about the Phantom Ship and the strange lights and noises they heard the night before.

CHAPTER 3

Riding the Big Horse

Later that afternoon, Gord went into the barn to get the bridle for the farm horse, as they were all planning on riding the big Strawberry Roan. The big horse was grazing on the abundant grass in the pasture behind the barn. Gord led the big horse, who was called Pal, over to the fence so that he could climb up and reach its big head to put the bridal on. The horse was as tame as a kitten and was very gentle with the kids. Adam and Molly joined Gord and climbed up on the fence so that they could get on his back. The horse was so big and so strong that the three kids could all ride around the pasture for hours at a time. Getting off sometimes posed a problem as the horses back was about seven feet off the ground. The usual routine was to bring him over to the fence, climb onto the fence, and get off that way. Today however, would be different. After walking and galloping around the pasture for a couple of hours, the big horse was working up quite a thirst and decided to head back to the barn for a drink out of the water trough in his stall. Gord pulled back on the reins and hollered, "Stop."

The horse's thirst was more important than listening to this young boy and he continued walking towards the barn door. The only problem facing the children was an eight foot high barn door and a seven foot back on the very large horse. Gord tried to make him turn, but the big horse's mind was made up as he lowered his head to go in the barn door.

"Quick everyone jump off!" shouted Gord.

Adam, Molly, and Gord all jumped off the left side of the horse, luckily landing in a big pile of hay that was beside the door.

"Is everyone all right?" said Gord.

"That was kind of fun," replied Adam.

"Luckily we didn't jump off the other side and land in that manure pile," said Molly laughing hysterically.

Gord went into the horse's stall and was able to take its bridal off while he was drinking. When Gord returned the bridal to the outer barn he overheard Tim talking to Uncle Almond who had come by to borrow the post hole auger.

Uncle Almond was saying that he had seen the Phantom Ship last night but that it had only been visible for a few short minutes and seemed to disappear beneath the surface of the water.

"Strange," said Tim, "Very strange and spooky."

Gord knew that they had to go out again that night. He just had to see what everyone was so afraid of.

All was quiet at the supper table except for talk of the bazaar and how fast Aunt Ann's cookies had disappeared so quickly when the baking tables opened.

Gord, Adam, and Molly decided that they would sneak

out that evening and continue their adventure. If only they could find the entrance to that cave again, they might find a clue to the mystery of the Phantom Ship.

Early that evening there were the sounds of rolling thunder in the distance. The crash of lightning bolts lit up the night sky and torrents of heavy rain fell on the farm. Three disappointed children sat in the playroom huddled around the big stone fireplace and made plans to try and find the cave the next day.

CHAPTER 4

The First Cave

Morning could not come quickly enough and as the sun was rising over the old red barn, three bright eyed children came up from the playroom eager to begin their adventure. After a quick breakfast of cereal and cinnamon buns Gord asked Mom if they could go down to the beach and collect shells. Mom and Aunt Ann agreed that it would be all right as long as they stayed out of the water considering they were not good swimmers and that the water would be too cold anyway.

The three set out and were soon scaling down the rocks to the beach. The sun was warm against their faces and they spent what seemed like hours trying to find the cave. They were about to give up when they spotted a scary black cat run down the beach and disappear into the rocks. Gord followed with his awkward gate and yelled over his shoulder, "It's here, this is it, the cave entrance, come on." Molly and

Adam arrived seconds later as they pushed back the rock that covered the entrance. Molly discovered something on the back of the rock; it was a skull and cross bones painted in white. They had not noticed it the first night as the rock had tipped backwards and the skull painting was facing the ground. Was this a clue to the Phantom Ship, or did it add confusion to the mystery?

"Let's explore the cave," Adam said. They crawled along the cave, familiar from two nights prior. Nothing was unusual as they reached the opening at the other end.

The entrance was damp and the walls were wet from the spring run off. These were the same walls that reflected the eerie light just two nights ago. The children retreated and came back to the end where they had come in. Adam decided that he would explore the other walls of the cave. Nothing seemed out of the ordinary until he came to the back corner of the cave. An opening to who knows what presented itself, at the top of the cave, about 8 feet off the cave floor. Stalactites hung from the roof restricting the opening. There seemed to be a very small opening that could be accessed by someone the size of Molly. Adam and Gord looked at Molly and urged "Come on, you can do it, don't you want to know what's behind there?"

Molly, very scared and unimpressed, shouted "I'm not going in there!"

After much pleading and begging and just enough tweaking of her curious nature, Molly gave in.

"Boost me up," she said. Gord boosted her up and she was on the ledge of the opening.

"Give me your flashlight," she demanded of Adam. Molly turned on the flashlight and peered in. Suddenly she screamed a horrifying cry and fell backwards as a large frightening bat flew by her head.

"That's it!" she cried, "I am not going in there!"

Adam figured if they brought back a shovel they could make the opening bigger, but what excuse could they use not to be suspicious. Gord said that he had seen people digging for clams last year. Maybe that could work.

CHAPTER 5

Digging for Clams

When the children arrived back at the farm, Aunt Ann asked, "So, where are all of your shells?" Adam said, "Oh, we sold them to a couple of tourists from Quebec City who hadn't much luck in finding good ones. We can always get more tomorrow Aunt Ann." Gord asked Uncle Rob if they could borrow a shovel to dig for clams. Uncle Rob said, "Sure, but good luck with that, they are usually too deep this time of the year."

Molly was tired and still quite spooked from the bat so she decided that she did not want to *dig clams* and would help mom and Aunt Ann with supper.

Adam and Gord headed back to the beach with shovel in hand. When they arrived at the cave they went in and Gord pushed Adam up to the ledge. Adam then pulled

Gord up with some difficulty. It was not long before they were knocking stalactites from the ceiling of the cave. This noise seemed to disturb the bats and several flew by them and out of the cave's entrance.

After the boys caught their breath, the two continued chipping away at the entrance, until the opening was large enough to gain entry. Gord cautiously went first through the opening, followed closely by Adam. Once through the aperture, the boys felt a cold dampness roll across the back of their necks and down their spines. They shivered more from fright than cold and held tight to each others' hands. Gord led the way for he wanted Adam to think that he was brave.

The first step brought a noise of snapping twigs. Adam shone the flash light to where the noise came from and let out a shriek. The twigs that they had heard snapping, were the bones of a hand, grey and brittle from years of immobility and deterioration. As Adam shone the light around, he and Gord could see more skeletal bones and old remnants of clothing that littered the floor of the cave.

What had they found? Was this the cave of the pirates? What else was here? Was there lost treasure? They *had* to know. It was nearing supper time and they would soon be missed at the supper table so they decided to head back to the farm. When the boys came back from the beach, Uncle Rob said, " Humm, no clams, ah I told you they were too deep. Oh well, you sure got dirty digging for those little suckers, go wash up for supper then."

Molly was anxious to find out what the boys had discovered, but had to wait until later that night. Molly suggested they tell Uncle Rob and Aunt Ann what they had discovered but the boys had other intentions.

"No, not now anyway, Uncle Rob and Aunt Ann probably wouldn't believe us or allow us to go to the beach again." Adam said. "You saw the looks on their faces when we mentioned the Phantom Ship. I say we keep this a secret until we know more. O.K?" he continued.

CHAPTER 6

Molly Sees the Light

The children were pretty tired and decided that they would wait until morning to investigate. That night however, shortly after midnight, Molly awoke with an uneasy feeling. She wasn't sure why. She walked to the window to look out in hopes of seeing something exciting. In the far off distance Molly saw a light which seemed to be sitting on the water of the bay. The light intensified and appeared to be a campfire gently cascading sparks. It was as if someone had thrown green sappy wood onto it. This was followed by very, very faint cries, which easily could have been missed, had it not have been so late and quiet. Was this the Phantom Ship? Could it be a bonfire on the distant shore? Who would know? How could she tell?

Molly wanted to run and awaken Gord and Adam, but she didn't want to miss a minute of this spectacular, but eerie show.

As she watched, a mysterious feeling came over her. "What is happening?" Molly thought. "I wonder if Aunt Ann, Uncle Rob, Tim and Uncle Almond all feel this way too? They have a fear for this strange illusion... this Phantom Ship that seems to haunt them."

Molly shivered at the thought, as the light of this strange occurrence faded and sunk into the surface of the water and disappeared into the calmness of Chaleur Bay.

That night, Molly had a very restless sleep with nightmares of the Phantom Ship haunting her dreams; only this time, the dying pirates were screaming her name. "Molly, help us Molly!" they cried.

CHAPTER 7

A New Life

It was morning now and at breakfast Molly was unusually quiet. Her mom asked if there was anything wrong and as Molly was about to spill her guts Uncle Rob stormed through the front door.

"Come quick kids," he said. "Old Bessie is having her calf." The kids briefly forgot about the Phantom Ship and followed Uncle Rob to the barn where they watched the miracle of life happening. Old Bessie mooed and with a big grunt, pushed the baby calf out on the straw covered barn floor. Old Bessie licked the calf from head to hoof and soon the little calf was standing on wobbly feet and suckling its mother.

"Wow, that was so neat," exclaimed Molly.

Uncle Rob looked proudly at Molly and he asked "Molly would you like to feed the calf from a bottle later? Seems as if Old Bessie is not producing enough milk."

Adam and Gord on the other hand, were not nearly

as excited about this new life. They decided to go and raid Aunt Ann's pantry for a snack. They were growing boys after all.

Right then and there the scary memories faded away as Molly cuddled the new born calf. It sucked on Molly's fingers until Uncle Rob gave her a bottle of warm milk. Old Bessie was quite comfortable with her new found baby sitter and she lied down and rested while her calf was being looked after. Molly spent the better part of the morning with the new calf; she stroked its forehead and scratched it behind the ears. She had found a new pet.

"Would you like to give her a Name?" asked Uncle Rob.

"Wow could I call her Buttercup? Asked Molly. She hugged the little calf and stroked its little head.

"Buttercup is a great name," said Uncle Rob.

"So Buttercup it will be," said Molly. She hugged the little calf and a large smile crept across her face.

Uncle Rob told her that she could come back later and visit, but now she had to let Buttercup spend some bonding time with its mother.

CHAPTER 8

Exploring the Cave

Molly opted to not go exploring that afternoon, and decided to stay with her new found companion instead. Adam and Gord, not as interested in the newly born calf, wanted to go and find more shells down at the beach since there were no chores to do. The boys made their way once again with shovel and bucket in hand, after convincing their mom to let them go and explore.

By now, the cave was quite easy to find. Adam had even remembered to bring some rope in order to climb up onto the ledge, considering the trouble he had pulling Gord up the last time. As Gord was lowering himself down into the cave Adam reminded him not to step on the bones.

"Don't worry," said Gord, "That creeped me out the last time and I won't be doing that again."

The flutter of bat wings followed by an eerie hiss could

be heard all throughout the cave as several bats dropped from the ceiling and exited through the very opening that the boys had come in.

"I hate those dang bats," Gord exclaimed as he dove out of their path of flight.

"Come on, we have to find out what is in here," said Adam.

As they cautiously moved around the walls of the cave, Adam shone his flash light on some strange markings on the wall that looked like they had been etched there by a sharp object many years ago. The markings did not seem to make sense to the boys however. They resembled small sail boats with X's over them.

"Maybe the pirates were keeping score," Adam suggested. "Perhaps this is how many boats they captured, and these bones are all that remains of the lost souls," he continued.

"But, but, there are almost a hundred boats here with markings. Why do these 2 not have X's through them? What does that mean?" stammered Gord.

"Maybe it's unfinished business."

"Maybe the ghosts of the pirate ship are coming back to finish what they started."

"Who could they be after?"

"I hope the heck it's not us."

"No, it must be something or someone a lot older than us. After all, these pirates lived many, many years ago," Adam replied.

"I wonder if there is a treasure map or some treasure around these caves. By the looks of these markings, it seems as though someone was looking for something. We could be RICH," Gord responded excitedly.

After another hour of searching the cave and finding

nothing except piles of bones, shreds of clothing, and part of what seemed like a buckle from an old shoe, the boys decided to call it a day. They left the rope inside the entrance of the cave, picked up a few shells on the way back to the farm as not to look suspicious, and pondered what the X's represented that were carved on the wall.

CHAPTER 9

Eclipse of the Moon and a Treasure Chest

That night at the dinner table Molly dominated the conversation recounting every possible detail of her day's experience with the new calf that she had named Buttercup. She was growing healthy and strong and spent more time with Molly frolicking in the fields than with Old Bessie.

Adam and Gord decided that they would go down to the beach and see if they could find more clues to the mystery of the Phantom Ship.

That night there was supposed to be a partial eclipse of the moon and only little convincing was needed to get permission to stay down at the beach late from Mom. Molly said that she did not want to go and after a few days of her turning down the opportunity to explore, Adam began to notice strange, spooky strange, and nervous strange in Molly ever since that night that she had seen the Phantom Ship.

Aunt Ann had packed them a few snacks and gave the children Uncle Rob's binoculars with a stern warning, "Don't lose these or Uncle Rob will be as mad as a wet hen."

The boys set out on their journey across the steep rocks, they climbed down carefully. They walked along the beach taking time to skip stones on the mirror like surface of the bay. It was ghostly quiet that evening as the sun was slowly setting casting its shimmering light onto the surface of the tranquil bay.

"Come on Adam," said Gord, "There is so much to do."

As they came to the entrance of the cave the boys encountered the same black cat that they had seen earlier. Now it was fighting with the sea gull over a fish that the gull had caught. The gull had been eating its catch near the entrance of the cave when the cat came flying through the air and viciously attacked the gull. The gull narrowly escaped and flew off leaving the trophy to the victor. The cat picked up the fish, hissed at the boys and darted back into the cave along the narrow tunnel until it felt that it was a safe distance to enjoy its stolen meal.

"There is something weird about that cat," said Adam as he crawled through the entrance, along the wall and up to the place where the little boats with the X's were.

This score sheet occupied Adam's mind a lot lately. Had they planned all of these mysterious encounters? Were they not random events? Did they know where and when the fishing vessels and pleasure crafts were going to be or did they just scratch a boat and put an X through it. But if that were so, then why did two boats not have X's through them?

Gord and Adam crawled up the rope to the ledge that they had left the last time and slid down being very careful not to step on the piles of skeleton bones. Adam turned his flashlight on and was surveying the walls when he tripped over something on the floor. He shone his flashlight down to where he had stumbled and was shocked at what he found.

"Look Gord," Adam said, "It seems to be the corner of an old trunk or a treasure chest," as his voice filled with excitement. "Come on and help me dig."

The boys used a sharp rock and Adam's pocket knife to scrape around the edges of the box.

"Where is that darn shovel when you need it? Said Gord. Finally after about an hour of scraping and scratching, the chest was free.

"Dang it, look at the size of that lock, we'll never get it open."

The chest wasn't very heavy and it did not seem like there would be much hidden treasure inside. The boys both pondered what could be in it that was so valuable to warrant such a huge lock.

"I bet Uncle Rob has a hack saw," said Adam.

Sadly we don't have time to get it now. We should wait and watch for the Phantom Ship tonight," he continued.

Gord was digging in the sand just outside the caves entrance to pass the time, as the sky darkened. He enjoyed digging straight down until he had a hole the length of his arm. The sun was setting on the bay and it would be an hour or so before the eclipse of the moon would be visible. The boys waited patiently as Gord continued to dig.

"What's this?" Gord called out as he pulled a little metal box out of the sand.

"Quick, open it," cried Adam. The box was quite rusted and fell apart in his hand, revealing a large iron key.

"You don't suppose that this is the key to the chest?"

"Come on, let's try it."

The boys rushed back inside the cave and carefully slid the key into the lock of the old chest. A turn and a click later and the lock sprang open. After fumbling awkwardly with the hasp, the chest was finally open. Adam reached in and pulled out a wooden ball about the size of a ping pong ball. Upon further examination, he found that it had a brown eye painted on one side of it. Adam had read that before glass eyes were invented, peoples' damaged eyes were replaced with wooden ones, but this dated back hundreds of years.

A large silver skull ring that must have come off a rather large finger was also in the chest. The only other treasures that the boys found were another key similar to that found in the sand and a piece of leather with a boat drawn on it in charcoal. Strangely enough, this boat was very similar to the ones on the cave walls that Adam had referred to as the score sheet.

"This is becoming more confusing by the minute," Adam exclaimed.

"What can all this mean?" said Gord.

It was starting to get dark and the early stages of the eclipse of the moon were beginning to show. It was spectacular, especially since this was the boys' first eclipse. Every now and then the boys would cast their eyes along the horizon hoping to get a glimpse of the Phantom Ship but as of yet, they were unable to experience what it was that Molly had seen nights before. The eclipse was finally over and Adam was beginning to yawn.

"Well, I think that we are out of luck tonight," replied Gord. "Let's call it a night and go home."

"We'll have to come back tomorrow and see if we can find the chest that belongs to that other key," said Adam.

CHAPTER 10

The Wooden Eye

Adam and Gord wondered about the ring, the key, the wooden eye and the piece of leather that they had found the night before. Where did they come from? Who did they belong to and more importantly, how did all of this tie in with the Phantom Ship... Or did it? The boys pondered for some time and decided that they needed to talk to Uncle Rob and see if he could answer some, or all of these questions.

The next morning at breakfast Aunt Ann asked if they had enjoyed the eclipse the night before and both boys agreed that it was quite the show, while keeping the treasures they found a secret.

After breakfast was all finished and cleaned up, Adam and Gord went out to the barn where Uncle Rob was fixing the thrasher.

"Uncle Rob," said Adam. "Did people use wooden eyes before glass eyes were invented?"

"They sure did," replied Uncle Rob. "Funny you ask, in fact your great grandfather Benjamin had one after his hunting accident. The cap of his musket sent a piece of metal into his eye and blinded him in one eye. Why do you ask Adam?"

"No reason," replied Adam.

"What ever happened to our great grandpa Uncle Rob?" Gord asked.

"His fishing boat went down many years ago and his body was lost at sea, or that is how the story goes since his boat was never found".

"Could this wooden eye be his?" Thought Gord.

Things were starting to fall into place. The pieces of the puzzle were starting to fit together and the boys' excitement was really starting to build. No wonder the mention of the Phantom Ship sent chills and frightened expressions across the faces of Uncle Rob and Aunt Ann. Maybe just maybe, the pirates had captured and killed their great grandfather. So many questions went through Adam and Gord's minds as they continued to uncover the story of the Phantom Ship - Should they show the wooden eye to Uncle Rob? How did the key and the leather fit into the puzzle? What was the key for anyway? Could there possibly be more than one chest?

As the kids helped with the barn chores that morning, their imaginations ran wild with possibilities of that might be unlocked with the secret key. They were running out of vacation time and with only a few days left to solve the mystery of the Phantom Ship, they knew they had to hurry.

CHAPTER 11

A Picnic at the Beach

That afternoon Aunt Ann had a picnic planned, so mum, Aunt Ann, and Uncle Rob piled into the cab of the old white, rust covered pick up truck and the kids pilled into the back. The beach was their destination and this pleased the kids to no end. Today they would not have to make up stories in order to go to the beach, and with a glimmer of hope, they might be able to uncover more of the mystery. After parking the truck, Aunt Ann and mum unpacked the picnic lunch of chicken salad sandwiches, giant raisin cookies and Kool Aid.

After some idle chit-chat about nothing in particular, Gord suggested that they go exploring on the beach. This met with mum's approval, and she sent the boys off to carry on their business. After all, it would give her and Aunt Ann some time to bathe in the sun and catch up on some much needed girl time.

Gord and Adam set on their way but before they could get too far Molly yelled "Wait for me guys. I'd like to come with you." Gord looked at Adam and said, "Why not, come along then."

The three hurried up the beach to their secret cave. There at the entrance of the cave was the mysterious black cat. She was hissing and scratching at what seemed to be some invisible intruder. She was jumping, lashing out, biting, hissing and snarling. Then after a few short seconds, she stopped and walked calmly into the cave as if the battle was over, and nothing had happened.

"That is one spooky cat!" exclaimed Molly.

"What the heck was she fighting with?" Asked Gord.

They all very slowly and cautiously entered the cave, while watching for this insane cat as Adam described it.

"Let's see if we can find the cat," said Molly.

"I think she might know something that could lead us to some more clues."

As they looked around the cave, it did not take long to discover the cat. She was sitting on top of the eight foot ledge leading to the inner cave. She seemed to be playing with something, batting it around and throwing it up into the air. What was it that she was playing with? Dare they get closer? What if she attacked? The boys decided that it would be safer to watch from a distance.

Molly's curiosity was getting the best of her however, as she inched closer and closer towards the creepy black cat. She slowly crept towards the cat until she was at the bottom of the ledge where the rope was hanging down. Suddenly, the cat stopped playing and jumped to the edge of the ledge while peering down at Molly. There was a terrifying moment of silence as Molly slowly and carefully crept backwards, keeping her eyes on the cat. The cat's eyes were drawn narrow and the hair on her arched back stood up as she gave a blood curdling hiss.

Molly screamed in terror and ran behind Gord, clutching tightly to his arm. The cat, satisfied that she had scared off this intruder, went back to playing and batting around the small object.

"What is that thing she is playing with anyway?" asked Molly. "It seems to sparkle and shine".

The children watched this mysterious animal play with the shiny object for a few minutes longer until she lost interest and jumped down from the ledge and ran out the door of the cave.

"Quick, let's see what she was playing with." said Gord.

He scrambled up the rope to the ledge like an experienced mountain climber.

"Wow, look at this," he exclaimed, as he held up a ruby set in a gold setting. It was the size of a peanut.

"It must be worth a fortune," Adam said.

"I wonder if it is real, or if there is more".

"What should we do with this beautiful jewel?" Asked Molly. "Should we give it to mum?"

"No, not at least yet, there is so much more that we have to find out," replied Adam.

The children had the leather piece with the boat on it, the wooden eye, the skull ring and now a ruby, but they wondered what would be next? Where was this leading them? To the true mystery of the phantom ship, or was this just a series of coincidences that would leave them with a simple memory?

"Let me see that," Molly exclaimed. The gold setting that held the ruby in place was very fascinating for the young girl. It looked like two very tiny hands holding the ruby closely and assuring not to drop it.

"It's so, so beautiful," She continued. "It must have

belonged to someone very special. I think I'll call it, Ruby's Hands".

"Let's get back to the picnic. Mom is going to be wondering where the heck we are," said Gord.

As they reached the blanket the children heard their Aunt Ann say, "What have you scallywags been up to?" but before any details could be spilled, Gord said "Oh Nothing much, let's eat, I'm famished".

CHAPTER 12

The Family Album
and Ruby's Hands

L ater on that evening, Uncle Rob was looking through his father's family album when Molly walked in.

"Whatcha doing Uncle?" asked Molly.

"Come on over here and I'll show you some pictures of your great grandfather in his army uniform," he said.

The two of them turned page after page of old black and white pictures stuck down with little black triangle picture holders, while Molly sat in the lap of her Uncle. After some time of stories and questions by Molly they came to a picture of a very elegantly dressed woman who Molly thought was so beautiful.

"Who is that?" she asked.

"She Molly, is your great grandmother. Isn't she beautiful?" Uncle Rob said.

Molly was about to turn the page when something caught her eye. There, hanging around the neck of her great grandmother was the 'Ruby's Hands'. Molly's heart stopped momentarily as she asked, "Uncle Rob, where is that beautiful necklace now?"

"Oh, I'm not sure sweetie. After your great grandmother died, your grandfather carried it in his pocket as a reminder of her and the love the two shared. He said it brought him luck on his fishing boat."

Molly was extremely confused as to what she should do. Should she show Uncle Rob 'Ruby's Hands' or should she just keep it a secret until the children had a better understanding of what they had been searching for? Molly kept it a secret for now, gave her Uncle a hug, and asked if she could show the pictures to Adam and Gord.

"Of course you can, just be very careful not to tear the pictures as they are very old and brittle you know," said Uncle Rob.

Molly went to the playroom where the boys were playing a game of chess.

"Look at this picture. On the neck of this beautiful woman is the treasure we found today. She is wearing "Ruby's Hands" said Molly excitedly, in a voice that was barely a whisper.

"Who is this?" asked Gord.

"It's our great grandmother who died many years ago. After she passed on, our great grandfather carried it with him for good luck when he went fishing. Don't you see, the pirates must have killed him and stolen the ruby," said Molly with a lot of sadness in her voice.

Adam pointed to another picture of their great grandmother in her garden and exclaimed, "Look beside the daisies. There is that black cat! You don't suppose it is the same cat we've come across?"

"No it's not possible." Gord added, "They say a cat has nine lives, but do you think that is true?"

"Maybe that wooden eye that we found belonged to great grandfather. Do you think the pirates took it when they stole 'Ruby's Hands'?" said Molly.

"What would they want with a wooden eye?" asked Adam.

"Who knows," replied Gord. "This mystery of the Phantom Ship is becoming more interesting by the minute."

They continued to look through the pictures and with Adam's sharp eye, another clue was found.

"Look at that big ring on great grandpa's finger," he said. "Molly, run up and see if Aunt Ann has a magnifying glass."

Molly hurried up the stairs and soon returned with a large black handled magnifying glass. Adam focused the glass on the ring and as sure as the sun rises every day, there it was: the skull ring that they had found just days before, along with the wooden eye and the key.

They turned the next page and there was a small picture missing. Only the four triangle corner holders stood by themselves. "I wonder what picture used to be in that spot," Molly wondered.

It was getting late so Molly took the album back to Uncle Rob, hugged him again and ran off to bed. Molly had trouble sleeping that night however. Just as she would start to drift asleep, the dreaded nightmares of pirates yelling, screaming and swinging their swords at her great grandpa, invaded her dreams and she would wake up trembling and sobbing. She felt like screaming out but she held it back in fear that she would have to tell what the nightmares were about.

CHAPTER 13

Psycho Cat and
the Second Cave

After helping Uncle Rob with the morning chores and saying goodbye to Buttercup the calf who was already starting to grow and become more independent. Molly chased her around the pasture one more time and then headed out for the beach with the boys. Adam brought the key just in case they found something to unlock the mystery of the Phantom Ship.

The three musketeers wanted to see if they could uncover any more clues to the mystery of the Phantom Ship. After all there was still the mysterious key. What would it open and where would they find it? If they ever could...

They started their journey in the usual way, concocting some believable story as to why they wanted to go to the beach. Today it was to search for driftwood. Tim, the hired hand, gave them ten cents for each piece of driftwood that he could turn into souvenir sail boats. After telling Mom about their opportunity and getting the go ahead to return to the beach, the children packed a lunch and headed for the beach. They climbed down the rocks while being careful not to fall and continued along the shoreline where the waves lapped against the rocks and up the beach to the pirate cavern.

Today the cat was lying on her back sunning herself, ignorant to the fact that three strangers were about to invade her domain. The children stopped and stood very still, suddenly the cat sprung to her feet and cried a loud teeth baring hiss and then growled through the very depths of her throat and darted into the cave.

"I'm not going in there," cried Molly as she started to run up the beach.

"Molly, come back," Adam called.

Molly turned to call back and tripped over a large piece of driftwood firmly rooted into the sand. The root looked like an arrow which was pointed to some very large rocks.

"Come on guys, this driftwood is telling us something," cried Molly.

They all ran towards the rocks and discovered an opening that led to an opening too small to get through. Its entrance was large enough to accommodate a cat perhaps, but too small for even Molly to squeeze into. Adam came to the conclusion that this was Psycho Cat's domain. Adam remembered back to his grade five science unit on simple machines. He recalled that one could move large objects using a pole and fulcrum and force arm. Gord being the scavenger he is, found a rather large tree trunk about three inches in diameter and eight feet long. With this, the children positioned the trunk under the large rock at the caves entrance and all pushed down on the log as hard as they could. With a few attempts Adam, Gord, and Molly were able to move the boulder – quite a bit easier than they had expected.

"It pays to listen in school. Sometimes you actually learn some useful stuff," said Adam.

Inside there was a tunnel big enough to crawl through but once again, the children were unsure of where it would lead them. Molly took one look at the size of the tunnel and said, "I'm not going in there, I don't want to meet Psycho Cat in a small tunnel like that. She would rip my eyes out and then I would have to get wooden ones like great grandpa."

Gord looked cautiously down the tunnel and said to Adam, "It looks like about fifty feet down and then the tunnel turns into a large opening. If we crawl real fast it should only take us about thirty seconds. Are you game?"

"You go first, I'll follow," replied Adam cautiously.

"What about me? You can't leave me out here alone," sobbed Molly.

"Then you better start crawling with us," exclaimed her brother Gord.

They all scampered through the tunnel like hamsters in a maze. Eight seconds later they appeared at the entrance of a fairly large cave. Molly described it as bigger than her bedroom, but smaller than the playroom. In one corner there was a pile of straw that was the perfect size for a cat's bed.

"I guess we are invading the Psycho Cat's Cave," said Gord.

Molly folded her hands and dropped to her knees while looking up to the roof of the cave.

"God, please keep Psycho Cat away while we are here, Amen" Molly prayed. Adam looked around and shone his light. To the right of the cat bed was a pile of old bones, and even further to the right, there were more boats on the wall with X's through them. This time only one was without an X. As the flashlight continued its trip further around the cave, it suddenly fell on an old wooden door with a big old rusty pad lock.

"Do you suppose this is it? Get your key Adam, hurry before the cat comes back," said Gord excitedly.

Adam carefully placed the key in the old rusty padlock and turned it. Suddenly, click, clack, clunk and the padlock fell open and landed on the ground.

"Be careful when you open the door, you never know what might be lurking behind or waiting to pounce on you," said Molly.

Gord, being the oldest and bravest of the group, said, "I'm not afraid," and cautiously started to pull open the wooden door. It was very heavy and the hinges let out an eerie squeak that sent shivers down his spine causing goose pimples to appear on his arm.

"That door needs some grease," said Adam as they all laughed.

It was just what they needed to relax their trembling bodies. As Gord pulled on the huge door, they heard a loud irritating and somewhat frightening, "Caw, Caw" as a huge black crow flew down the narrow tunnel behind the door. He was half flying and half hopping in the narrow sections.

"So the door concealed another mysterious tunnel but I wonder where it leads?" questioned Adam.

"Follow that crow," said Gord.

They all started down the tunnel, first Gord, then Adam, and lastly, Molly followed clinging onto Adam's sweater. The crow stopped now and then, as if to let them catch up. He started to squawk and chatter. It was then that they noticed, the crow was missing one eye.

"This keeps getting stranger by the minute," Molly suggested.

"I think the crow is trying to tell us something," Adam thought out loud.

The one eyed crow uttered a mixture of caws and shrieks and flew off down the tunnel. The children followed him tentatively. Soon the tunnel opened into a larger cave.

"It is about the size of Aunt Ann's kitchen," said Molly. This made her think of aunt Ann's delicious cinnamon buns.

The crow continued his squawking and flew to a dark corner of the cave where he landed on an old wooden trunk. He cautiously looked around sizing up the children while walking back and forth across the trunk - almost military style - constantly keeping his good eye in their direction.

"He is guarding whatever is in that trunk," suggested Gord.

"What do we do? Should we wait him out, or try to scare him away?" asked Adam.

"I'm not going to scare him away," said Molly. "He freaks me out with that big black sharp beak and one spooky eye," she continued.

They watched the crow for a short while until suddenly he squawked and cawed, and flew out of the cave, just missing their heads.

"There must be another way out, reasoned Adam.

"There is no way that the crow could live locked up in here," added Gord.

Being his inquisitive self, Adam wandered around the opening and shown his flashlight around the walls. Upon further investigation he discovered a small crow sized hole near the top of the cave where a glimmer of sunlight shone through.

"That must be where he escapes from," Adam muttered to himself.

"Let's look in the trunk," suggested Gord.

There was another padlock on this trunk that was large and rusted. It looked different than the ones they had seen in their books.

"Try your key Adam," suggested Molly.

Adam fumbled in his pocket for the key, and gently placed it into the lock. He turned it with a flick of his wrist but sadly, nothing happened. This was not the right key.

"Now what?" questioned Gord.

"Well, we cannot do anything without a key. so let's see where that crow size hole leads." Adam exclaimed.

The boys pushed the trunk over underneath the hole and stood it on its end so that they could reach the opening.

"This isn't very heavy," exclaimed Gord.

"I wonder what is inside?" questioned Adam.

Adam climbed up on the trunk and looked out the hole in the rocks.

"Nothing special up here," he said.

He noticed that the sun was high in the sky and figured they should be getting back to the farm. Gord suggested that they go back and spend the afternoon at the farm and come back in the evening to see if they could spot the Phantom Ship. They picked up a few choice pieces of driftwood for Tim so that no one would be suspicious of their adventure. When they arrived back at the farm and took the wood to Tim, he thanked the kids and paid them a combined dollar and a quarter.

Tim said, "You guys sure didn't find much for the amount of time you were gone, but I appreciate the effort so I gave you a little extra." The children all smiled at each other knowingly that their adventure had really just begun.

CHAPTER 14

Old Ben

That afternoon, Molly was out at the barn visiting Buttercup, who was growing bigger by the day when suddenly she heard that very memorable "Caw Caw". Molly looked up and saw the one eyed crow sitting on top of the barn looking down at her.

"Uncle Rob, why does that crow only have one eye?" Molly asked. "We saw it down at the beach earlier today," she continued.

"That's old Ben," said Uncle Rob.

"Old Ben...who is Old Ben?" asked Molly.

"Come here and let me tell you a story," said Uncle Rob.

"You see Molly, most people think that when you die you go to Heaven or Hell, but some people believe in reincarnation. This means that when you die you come back to earth as another being or possibly an animal. The belief is that your life does not end rather you begin a new journey as another creature. Your great grandfather Benjamin believed in reincarnation and so did your great grandmother Ruby".

"You mean that my great grandma's name was Ruby!" exclaimed Molly.

All this time Molly and her brothers were thinking that the pendant they found, and that Molly named "Ruby's Hands" had way more significance than they had ever imagined.

"Yes, your great grandmother's name was Ruby," Uncle Rob continued, "Anyway, your great grandfather as I told you before, had only one eye and the other was wooden. He was a cranky old man and always complained about something. It was too rainy or too hot, or too much snow or not enough rain to plant the crops. Your great grandma Ruby would say that he was a crotchety old crow and would nag that he complained too much. Anyway, shortly after your great grandpa Ben went missing at sea and we assumed was lost, this old one eyed crow started hanging around the farm as if he was keeping an eye on us to make sure the farm was being looked after properly. Your grandfather started calling the crow Old Ben. He always sat on the barn and cawed out his complaints or comments," said Uncle Rob.

"That's absolutely fascinating," said Molly. "Do you think that old crow is really great grandpa Ben?" continued Molly.

Just then Old Ben flew down and landed in front of them and hopped up onto the tractor seat. He looked at Molly with his good eye and Molly swore that he winked at her, before he let out a friendly caw and flew off towards the beach.

"You know Molly, no one really knows what happens when someone dies but it's kind of nice to think you could come back and see your loved ones again even if they didn't know it was you."

Molly couldn't wait to share her new found knowledge

with Gord and Adam. She dashed off to the house to tell the boys about Old Ben after giving her Uncle a hug and a kiss, and saying a few quick words to the baby calf. Molly found them in the playroom discussing the Phantom Ship.

"Guys I have something to tell you," she said. Then she told them the story about Old Ben the crow and that Ruby was the name of their great grandmother.

"Ruby's Hands?" questioned Adam.

"I know," said Molly smiling.

"Do you suppose that great grandfather Ben was killed by the pirates and Old Ben is trying to lead us to their treasure or better yet, the mystery of the Phantom Ship." said Adam as he raised his voice to his scariest pitch.

"But, remember the cat in the picture with great grandma Ruby, this cat could even be Ruby, don't you see," said Molly.

"Wow, this is getting so confusing," said Gord as he scratched his head. He then continued "let's sneak out tonight after everyone is asleep and find that Phantom Ship. Maybe the cat and the crow will help us."

That night after everyone was asleep Molly tiptoed down the hall and quietly crept down the stairs to the playroom where the boys were waiting for her. They grabbed their jackets and flashlights and quietly went out the back door and down the stone and gated road towards the beach. There were many dark clouds and the wind was cold. The children were far enough away from the farm house now so they put on their jackets, zipped them up tight to their necks and turned on the flashlights so they could see where they were walking and what it was that they may encounter. The wind was biting at their necks and ears however and the children wondered if they had made the right choice to sneak out.

Adam was in the lead as they shone their flashlights on the rocks and scaled their way down the banks.

"Let's go into one of the caves so that we can get out of this horrible wind," he said.

Adam's flashlight shone on the entrance of the cave where they had first seen the strange light on the wet walls. As they took a closer look the children realized that and two very bright and shiny objects shining back at them were the scary green eyes of the Psycho Cat.

Tonight the cat did not hiss or growl, rather she gave a long gentle meow and walked into the cave.

"Was that Jekyll and Hyde or what?" said Adam.

Molly had a puzzled look on her face so Adam explained that when the same person has two different personalities, often good and evil, he or she is called this.

"I think that cat is Great Grandma Ruby and she knows that we know about her and Ben so she is not threatened by us anymore," declared Molly.

The children sat on a log at the entrance of the cave just far enough inside to be out of the wind, but close enough to get a good view of the Bay. The moon was very bright when it was not hidden behind the eerie black and grey clouds.

"The moon seems to be telling ghost stories to the clouds," said Molly

"That's quite the imagination you've got there young lady," replied Gord.

"The sky looks like a scene from a movie just before something terrible happens and I'm scared," cried Molly.

Suddenly the moon dropped behind a cloud creating a mysterious halo around the cloud. The winds subsided and there was a dreary silence. Nothing could be heard except the beating of three very scared little hearts.

"Something horrible is going to happen. I just know it," cried Molly.

Suddenly the flapping of wings and that familiar Caw, Caw, broke the silence of the night air. Old Ben flew over their heads and up into the night sky towards the halo crested cloud. The children watched the crow until he disappeared into the clouds.

"Crows are usually low fliers and don't even like forests with tall pines, why would he fly away up there?" asked Adam.

"This is not your ordinary everyday crow, this is Old Ben," said Molly proudly.

It was getting late and the children were a little tired and kind of scared. Gord suggested that they call it a night and head back to the farm for some rest.

Just as they started to turn and walk away from the beach they heard the beating of wings and Old Ben landed not ten feet away from them.

"Look, he has something in his beak," said Adam. The crow dropped a large iron key, cawed and flew away.

"I wonder if that is the key to the last trunk that we found in the crows cave?" questioned Gord.

"Let's go home and we can check in the morning. It's after midnight and we should get some sleep," suggested Adam.

The walk back to the farmhouse seemed much longer as they were dragging their feet and yawning at the same time. Finally they arrived back at the house and saw a light in the kitchen window.

"Oh no, are we ever going to get in trouble now," said Molly

"Let's be real quiet and stay in the shadows and maybe

we can sneak in the back way like we came out," suggested Gord.

Everything went well and all were safe inside, but Molly had to sneak by the kitchen where Aunt Ann was having a cup of tea because she could not sleep. Molly peered around the corner of the door that came to the kitchen from the playroom. Aunt Ann seemed to be absorbed in the Sears spring catalogue and Molly crept by without being noticed.

CHAPTER 15

The Visitor

Molly had trouble falling asleep that night. She did not like sneaking around or hiding secrets from her family, but she knew that Mom and Aunt Ann would not let her and her brothers continue the search for the Phantom Ship if they knew what was going on.

After staring at the ceiling, trying to count sheep, and counting back from one hundred twice, Molly finally fell asleep, only to be awakened a short time later by a faint tapping on her window. She went over to the windowsill and saw a black shadow cast on her wall. She opened her mouth to scream, but when she realized what was causing the shadow she then put her hand over it quickly and prevented it from escaping.

"Old Ben, what are you doing here?" asked Molly.

Old Ben stepped inside the window and perched on the foot of the bed as he winked at Molly with his good eye. A warm feeling came over her. Old Ben had never been this close before and she was not the least bit afraid. Molly knew that the crow could not talk to her so she started to ask him questions with the hope that he would be able to give her some kind of answers.

"Are you Great Grandfather Ben?" she asked the one eyed crow.

Old Ben nodded his head up and down in response.

"Were you a pirate?" she continued.

Ben shook his head from side to side as if he were saying no.

"Did the pirates kill you?" Molly queried.

Ben, with a sad look in his one eye shook his head yes and this made Molly tear up a bit. Regardless of the truth she was finding out, she knew she needed to continue asking her Great Grandfather the questions that were burning in her and her brothers' minds.

"Do you know the mystery of the Phantom Ship?" she continued with a lump in her throat. Old Ben then threw up his wings as if to say, "I'm not sure."

"Can you help us solve the mystery Great Grandfather Ben?" pleaded Molly.

Old Ben shook his head up and down and flew out of the window. Molly slowly climbed back into bed as she pondered what had just happened. Again, it took her a long time to drift back to sleep while her mind raced with more questions about the Mystery of the Phantom Ship.

⌒

In the morning Molly awoke tired and dreary, not too sure if she had been dreaming or if the conversation she had with the crow was actually real. She walked over to the window and discovered a large black pinion feather lying on the floor. She knew then, that she had not been dreaming and in fact, the conversation with Old Ben *actually* occurred. Molly knew in her heart that Old Ben would indeed help them to uncover the mysteries behind the Phantom Ship.

Molly ran downstairs to tell Adam and Gord about her visitor in the middle of the night. The boys were still asleep in the playroom and she did not realise that she was still carrying the black feather. As Molly entered the kitchen for breakfast, and to wait for her brothers to wake up from their slumber, she was confronted by her Mom.

"Where did you get that big black feather?" Mom asked.

Molly stuttered for a moment and said, "It must have blown into my window last night while I was sleeping. It was on the floor this morning when I woke up" Molly replied.

"What are you going to do with it?"

"I'm going to keep it forever and ever. I just have a feeling that it is a very special feather," Molly said with a charming smile.

"Maybe it's one of Old Ben's feathers," said Uncle Rob while winking at Molly.

"Stop joking Rob, all that foolishness about Old Ben is just that, a bunch of foolishness," Aunt Ann said with a scolding tone in her voice.

Molly so wanted to agree with Uncle Rob and state her case that she was sure that the crow was really her Great Grandfather Ben, but she knew that her family would not believe such a presumption. She had so much proof including last night's visit and yet she was still unable to tell her family what it was that she, Adam, and Gord were up to during their visit. She felt that it was still important to keep her secret to herself so she just smiled and winked at Uncle Rob, waived her feather when Aunt Ann wasn't looking and Uncle Rob smiled back and returned the wink. Finally, around ten o'clock Adam and Gord stumbled upstairs.

"Help yourselves to some fresh fruit and cinnamon buns," Aunt Ann said to the boys. "Uncle Rob is already doing his morning chores and he might need some help," she continued.

CHAPTER 16

Ploughing the Fields

Uncle Rob had been up for hours and had already finished most of the chores before coming in for his mid morning coffee.

"Hey lazy bones, you two have already missed half the day. I'm going to help Tim put new shoes on the big Strawberry Roan and then we are going to do some ploughing. If you kids want to come along and ride on the horse's back while we plough, you can. It will only take a couple of hours," said Uncle Rob.

The kids decided that this could be a lot of fun, considering that there would still be time in the late afternoon, to go and find out what the crow's key was all about. They nodded their heads to Tim and Uncle Rob and said in unison, "We would be delighted!" The three children followed closely behind their uncle as he made his way to the barn.

Watching Tim and Uncle Rob put new horse shoes

on the big horse was something new for the kids. They had never seen this done before and it was a bit worrisome for Molly especially. Molly was quite concerned when Tim started to pound nails into the horse's hooves.

"Doesn't that hurt him, Uncle?" asked Molly with a note of concern in her voice.

"His hooves are like your nails. It does not hurt when you cut your nails, right?" asked Uncle Rob.

It did not take too long to finish shoeing the horse and then the children watched their Uncle hitch him up to the plough so they could turn over the sod in the field behind the barn. Molly and Adam climbed up on the big horse's back and Uncle Rob showed Gord how to steer the plough. He explained to Gord "If you want the horse to turn left, you call 'Gee' and if you want him to turn right you yell 'Haw'. Why don't you give it a try?"

Gord took the reins with hesitancy and walked the horse around the field while calling out 'Gee' and 'Haw'. To his surprise, he was able to steer the great big horse! After a while, Adam wanted to try steering too, so he and Gord traded places. Molly was content just to be along for the ride. They finished ploughing around three o'clock and asked if they could go to the beach for a little while.

Aunt Ann asked, "What is so interesting about the beach?" She then continued, "You spend so much time down there."

Adam was quick to reply, "It's a new adventure every day. New driftwood, new shells, shinny pebbles, and who knows what else, maybe a pirate's treasure." Then he laughed as Molly and Gord joined in, knowing that only the three of them shared the big secret.

CHAPTER 17

The Crow's Cave
Has Clues

A unt Ann agreed that there was a new adventure to be found and that the beach had a lot of interesting things. She allowed the children to go under the condition that they would be home before sunset. Adam, Gord, and Molly smiled at Aunt Ann and thanked her, while promising to be home before sunset. With a back pack to carry their found trinkets, they headed off to the beach, almost as fast as their legs could carry them.

Without a word, Molly and Adam followed Gord excitedly towards the unopened trunk in the crow's cave.

"What do you suppose is in that trunk?" Gord asked.

"I don't know, but whatever it is, it must not be treasure. This trunk is not heavy enough to be filled with gems," Adam said somberly.

At the entrance of the cave on a rock ledge, Old Ben sat pecking at the bones of an old fish, that the Psycho cat had left days earlier. He looked at them and bobbed his head up and down. Molly reached into her pocket and found some sunflower seeds that she had from when the children were ploughing earlier that day.

"Here Ben, these are for you, and I bet you will like them better than that old fish," she said as she tossed a handful into the crow's direction.

The children watched as Old Ben gobbled up the seeds, nodded his head in the direction of the trunk, and then flew away. Molly, Adam, and Gord all looked at each other with a familiar sense of excitement and gratitude for what they used to believe was a pesky crow. Now, even if it were only they who knew the secret, the children truly did believe that the crow was their long lost great grandpa Ben, and they would uncover his story with his help. With that in mind, the kids could not help their excitement building and continued on.

"I can't wait to see what's inside the trunk" said Adam. "Come on, let's go in and find out." he continued.

The children hurried on into the cave, but to their surprise, there was an unexpected visitor. There she was – Psycho Cat – but today, something was different about her. Instead of her regular hissing and snarling at them, she stretched out on her back, meowed a friendly meow, and then let out a warming purr, while curling up alongside a freshly eaten fish carcass.

"Why is she being so friendly today?" Gord wondered aloud.

"That cat is definitely Great Grandma Ruby!" exclaimed Molly.

"Maybe she's Grandma Ruby's cat, since they are said to have nine lives, you know," chuckled Gord.

"Enough time wasted with that silly cat," Adam said. "Let's get this trunk open and see what's inside!"

He fumbled around in his pocket for a few moments and found the key, along with a piece of blue lint and gum wrapper from earlier in the day. He gave the key a quick blow and sure enough, when he put it into the lock and turned it slowly, the lock popped open with a click. Adam opened the trunk lid as Gord and Molly looked over his shoulder with anticipation.

"All that work for a dusty old telescope," Molly sighed. "I was hoping for something much prettier!"

"I bet this telescope was used to spy on the pirates' next victims," Adam said as he held the telescope up to inspect it a little bit closer.

"Wait a minute, what is this?" Gord asked, as he picked up a paper with a faded and tattered, hand drawn map of the coast, on it.

"Are those the three caves that we have explored?" Adam asked, as he set down the telescope and took hold of the fragile paper. "Look! There is a little black boat in this cove and it has the same drawing as the other's we found on the wall. This one doesn't have an X though" he stated matter-of-factly.

"What does this mean?" Gord questioned.

Molly continued to dig through the trunk in hopes she would still find something pretty. The only other thing she found in the trunk, was a black leather eye patch. She handed it to Gord and he picked it up to examine it more closely. In the centre of the patch was a small white skull and cross bones, that had carefully been painted.

"Was this great grandpa Ben's eye patch? Do you think he was one of the pirates?" Adam asked. "This keeps getting more and more confusing."

"Old Ben would never steal from anyone, I just know

it in my heart," Molly scolded, as she crossed her arms and glared at Adam for even suggesting such an absurd thing.

"Don't you look at me like that Molly!" Adam sneered. "I am just trying to put the pieces together that we have found."

"Okay you two. That's enough bickering. We should get headed back to the farm anyway," Gord said.

The kids agreed to cut their adventure short, as it was getting close to supper time. They put the telescope, tattered map, and eye patch carefully into their backpacks, and zipped them up tightly. Adam slipped the key back into his pocket for safe keeping and they all made their way back to the farm

CHAPTER 18

Making Plans

Adam seemed very quiet at the supper table, as he was preoccupied with trying to analyse the strange map in his mind.

"Goodness gracious, what have you got on your mind boy? You seem to be far away in Never, Never Land," said Aunt Ann.

Adam thought for a moment and exclaimed, "I'm thinking about the Phantom Ship Auntie. There is just something about it that I cannot get out of my head. It seems as though there is more to it than people are led to believe."

"Never you mind about such foolishness," scolded Aunt Ann, as she turned around to hide the troubled look on her face.

Adam did not want to cause any more trouble. "I'm sorry for bringing it up Auntie. It's just such an interesting phenomenon. That's all. Thank you for making dinner.

This apple jelly sure is delicious with these pork chops," he continued with a charming smile.

Aunt Ann smiled back but still had an uneasiness about her. This intrigued Adam's sense of wonder even further and he nudged Gord under the table. After the supper dishes were cleared from the table, the children went downstairs to the playroom to discuss a plan of action. They opened up the little suitcase where they had been keeping all the clues that they had found. The wooden eye complete with a pirates eye patch, the compass, two keys, a skull ring, a piece of leather with the boat on it, Ruby's Hand pendant, a hand drawn map, and a telescope . They studied each item again and tried to make sense of the questions they had encountered.

Gord picked up the map and stared at it for a long time. His siblings could tell that he was deep in thought and allowed him a few minutes of silence. When they could see that Gord was ready, Adam asked "What do you make of it?"

"I don't exactly know," replied Gord, "but I bet the mystery lies within that boat. We have seen the caves and know what is in them. We have found the keys and clues, but there is no boat in that cove… At least not yet." reasoned Gord.

"Maybe that is where the pirates docked their ship, or maybe that is where the ghost of their ship lives," suggested Molly.

"I don't know about you guys, but I say we sneak out tonight and see if we can find the Phantom Ship," Adam stated. Gord and Molly nodded in agreement.

When it was time to get ready for bed, the children changed into their pajamas, brushed their teeth and said their goodnights to Mom, Aunt Ann, and Uncle Rob. They each made their way to bed and patiently, although anxious, waited for the house to become quiet. Time passed so slowly on this night as Molly, Gord and Adam all pondered what the phantom ship would look like or if they would even be able to uncover the mystery they had been hunting for several days.

When all the adults were asleep, the three children quietly snuck out and down the garden path to the beach, being careful not to shine the light too bright or to make any suspicious noises. The moon was bright and the boys did not feel the need for a light. Molly kept her flashlight on however, as she felt the bugs would stay out of the light and away from her feet. She detested the sound of crushed bugs.

The beach was very quiet, except for the distant cry of a seagull. The children could hear the gentle lapping of the water at the shoreline and the crunch of the sand beneath their feet. They walked along the shore line looking up at the moon occasionally, while being careful not to forget why they were out there so late at night.

"This is almost too quiet," Molly worried out loud.

The moon was sitting low in the sky and cast a glimmering light on the glassy smooth waters of the Bay. The children walked until they came to the cave closest to where the cove was, and spread out a blanket on the rocks. They sat and waited for something, or anything, to happen. It was not long before they heard a very familiar "Caw, Caw, Caw," in the distance and a short while later, Old Ben landed about ten feet away from their feet. He was agitated and nervously paced back and forth across the wet sand, leaving little imprints each time he stepped.

Molly reached in her pockets and threw him some more sunflower seeds while saying, "Easy big Fella" in a calming voice that she had heard Uncle Rob say to the big horse, earlier on. Old Ben ignored the seeds and kept looking out on the water with his good eye, as he continued to pace back and forth.

"Something really has Old Ben bothered!" Adam stated. "I wonder why he is so unsettled."

Suddenly, a dark cloud as black as night, swept in front of the moon and cast eerie shadows over the water. Old Ben let out another squawk and peered up toward the sky.

"I'm scared," cried Molly as she cuddled up to Gord. He put his arm around her and pulled the blanket up around her shoulders.

Everything went deathly quiet and suddenly a faint light seemed to break the surface of the Bay. As it seemed to rise out of the water the light grew brighter in intensity. Faint screams echoed across the water and the light grew and became fiery like.

"I wish we had brought that spyglass," said Gord as the light continued to intensify and began to look as though a ship was burning.

"Look! That's the Phantom Ship!" cried Adam. "You can see three distinct masts. We've finally found it!"

The flames continued to grow in size and brightness and the screams increased in volume and frequency. Large fire balls were flying off the burning ship and dying out as they faded below the surface of the water. Just as quickly as it had started, the screams faded to nothing and the flaming ship sunk beneath the surface of the bay. The three children sat in awe and horror of what they had just witnessed for themselves. Everything, including the children, was so quiet, that the only noise at all, was the rapid beating of three little hearts.

"That was truly amazing," said Adam.

"I would like to get a closer look and see what is really happening," replied Gord.

"Maybe next time we should bring the spyglass," suggested Adam.

Molly sat very quiet and appeared to be quite bothered. Gord noticed this and asked, "What's up Molly? What are you thinking about? But more importantly, are you O.K.? I know that was a lot to witness," he continued as he wrapped his little sister in a big and comforting hug.

Molly turned her head to one side and said, "I feel kind of funny – sort of scared and a little bit overwhelmed. I can understand why Uncle Rob, Aunt Ann and Tim all looked so weird when we mentioned the Phantom Ship. Knowing that there is a ghost ship out there and not having an explanation of why it comes back is very disturbing."

"You aren't wrong little sis'. This whole adventure has been a bit creepy. At least we are figuring it out together!" Gord assured her.

The children looked around to see if Old Ben was still with them, but all they found was one of his pinion feathers.

"It's so strange that none of us heard him fly away," said Adam.

"Maybe he just walked quietly into the cave," reasoned Molly. "You could tell that he was very nervous. Wouldn't you be nervous too if the pirates who killed you, came back after you were reincarnated, to haunt you some more?" Molly questioned with just a touch of sarcasm in her voice.

"You know, we had better get home and get some sleep before Uncle Rob gets up to start the chores," said Adam, as a slight shiver went down his spine. The whole experience of seeing the phantom ship bothered him as well, but he did not want his siblings to see that he too, was disturbed.

On the way back to the farm the children kept looking

back over their shoulders partially because they were curious and partially because they were scared. They snuck in the back door to the playroom and this time, Molly did not encounter any obstacles on the way back to her bedroom. She laid her head upon her pillow, looked up to the bright moon shining in her window, and drifted off to sleep quickly. She was exhausted – physically, mentally, and emotionally.

CHAPTER 19

Gone Fishing

Morning seemed to come much too soon and the three sleepy heads came into the kitchen for breakfast, while yawning and stretching.

"Didn't you kids get enough sleep last night?" Uncle Rob asked, while coming in from feeding the chickens and collecting the eggs for breakfast.

"Who wants bacon and fresh eggs?" bellowed Aunt Ann.

It was unanimous with the children as they had worked up good appetites with all the excitement from the night before. The smell of crackling bacon filled the air and the hot pan sizzled as aunt Ann cracked in egg after egg. Now the kids were getting really hungry. They helped to set the table as they made small talk with uncle Rob.

"Sure looks like a nice day outside," Gord remarked.

"How's Buttercup doing today, Uncle?" Molly asked.

"Oh, she's doing just fine Molly. Getting bigger and stronger each day," Uncle Rob replied.

"I sure am hungry now," Adam said, as he rubbed his belly.

"Well, you are just in luck. Breakfast is ready," Aunt Ann announced.

Uncle Rob had pretty much finished the daily chores and after eating a delicious breakfast, he asked if the kids would like to go fishing and take a picnic lunch. They had not spent a lot of time with Uncle Rob on this Easter Vacation so they decided to give the search for the Phantom Ship a wee rest and spend some quality time with their favourite uncle. The children all climbed into the old white pickup truck and in a few short minutes they were at the little fork in the river where it narrows and thins so much, that trout can be seen swimming around.

"Let's dig some worms out of the ground and catch some fish," said Uncle Rob clapping his hands with excitement.

They turned over a few rocks and dead logs, and dug with the little spade that Uncle Rob had brought along.

"Hey Uncle Rob, I found a whole bunch of worms in this patch of rocks. They are squirming around and every time I touch them, they feel slimy. Ugh," Molly said disgustedly. "Would you *please* put one on my hook for me?" she continued with her best puppy dog eyes. Adam came to Molly's rescue and then threaded the biggest wiggly worm he could find, onto his own hook. They he was the first to toss his line into the water and sheer moments later, he had a bite.

"Wow! That didn't take long," Adam said joyously.

"Well done my boy! Let's reel 'er in nice and slow," Uncle Rob said with a grin.

"We will only keep enough to have for supper and then

we will release the others back into the stream. This way, there will always be a fresh and bountiful supply of fish."

After about an hour, they had caught enough fish for supper and had released a few more back into the river. Molly put down a blanket and set out the picnic lunch that she had helped her mom make earlier that morning. They had made ham sandwiches with the crusts cut off, hard boiled eggs, celery and carrot sticks with a creamy dip, and a big pitcher of lemonade.

"You boys sure do stink! All of that fish, dirt, and worms... *Yuck!*" exclaimed Molly. "Why don't you go wash up before lunchtime?" she asked.

They agreed that it was a good idea as they rinsed their hands in the river and wiped them on their jeans. Everyone sat down on the soft blanket and felt the warm sun on their faces. As they were all enjoying their picnic lunch, Adam pondered how to ask Uncle Rob about the Phantom Ship and how to tell him that they know it exists. After all, they had seen it just last night. He did not know how to bring it up without getting in trouble for sneaking out of the house past their bedtime.

Adam continued to replay the words in his mind when suddenly, out of nowhere, Molly said, "Uncle, would you please tell us about the Phantom Ship? We really want to know more."

There was a long silence and Uncle Rob's face went blank of expression. Quietly, and in a low voice, he began. "The less you know about the Phantom Ship, the better you will be. Now let's just leave it at that. I really don't want to talk about it now."

Not much was said for the rest of the picnic. Soon it was time to hop back into the old white pickup truck and get back to the farm.

"Uncle, one night I woke up and saw something burning

on the bay, do you think that it was the Phantom Ship?" asked Molly.

"It was probably some college students building a bonfire on the beach" said Uncle Rob. "Please, enough about the Phantom Ship. O.K." he continued.

The kids could tell that Uncle Rob was upset so they did not talk much on the rest of the ride home.

CHAPTER 20

The Ring

It was mid afternoon and the children had some exploring to do so they made up some lame excuse for mom, to once again go down to the beach. With a reminder to come back before dinnertime, the children gave their mother a kiss and headed toward the gate. Gord, Adam, and Molly were all running down the beach but no one seemed to have a plan or know where they were going, or what they would do when they got down there.

"Wait a minute, guys, where are we going?" asked Molly.

"I don't know," said Adam "I was just following Gord."

"I think we have to check out the cove on the map and see if we can find any signs of a boat, or clues to what it might mean," Gord replied.

They started to run again and arrived at the cove in no time at all. Adam went to the edge of the shore and peered out onto the water, while using his hand to shield the sun's glare on his glasses.

"Let's wade into the water and see if we can find anything," Gord suggested.

He took off his shoes and socks, rolled his pant legs up, and started to venture in, only to find that the water was freezing cold. The children tried to see anything beneath the surface of the water that might be a clue; however, there was no evidence of old ship boards or anything that might suggest a boat was ever there.

"This is puzzling. Why is there a boat in the drawing?" Gord questioned.

Adam scratched his head, pushed his glasses up on his nose, and then looked up and to the left as he always did when he was deep in thought.

"We should come back here tonight and observe the Phantom Ship from this spot, and maybe, just maybe, we will discover something worthwhile," Adam responded.

"Tonight will be a great night to go since Mom, Aunt Ann and Uncle Rob are going into town to the square dance at the community hall. They said that they wouldn't be home until midnight," Gord said with a hint of excitement in his voice.

While they were on the beach, the children decided to explore the caves once again to see if they had missed any clues or hints, to help solve the mystery.

Molly did not want to go into the cave with the bones again. She pleaded "Please don't make me go back in there. If I step on anymore bones, I'll scream so loud that your guys' ear drums will break."

They boys looked at each other and chuckled a bit. "How about you wait for us out here Molly? I'm sure the sea gulls will keep you company," Adam snickered.

She decided to do just that and had a seat on a rock at the entrance of the cave. She looked around the sandy beach, across the water, and then watched the sea gulls and gannets dive for minnows.

Molly was enjoying the sun and watching the clouds go by as she lay in the warm wet sand. She tried to find as many animals in the clouds as she could, and made stories up in her head as she found each new animal. She had just started to doze off, when she felt something rub up against her shoulder. She turned her head slowly and was about to scream, yet nothing came out. The hair on the back of her neck stood up instead. There, leaning up against her, was Psycho Cat. This time she was not hissing or growling or snarling. She did not have an arched back or a mean look about her. Rather, a soft purr radiated from her warm body. Molly very cautiously rolled onto her side and offered her hand. The cat rubbed her head on the back of Molly's hand. She meowed softly and scampered off about twenty feet away, only to stop and look over her shoulder and meow again.

"Hey guys, come here quick," Molly bellowed into the cave. "The psycho cat wants us to follow her," she continued. Molly could hear foot steps and bones crunching beneath her brothers' feet. She shuddered a bit and shouted "Hurry up! I have something to tell you."

As the boys emerged from the cave, squinting at the blindingly bright sunlight, Gord asked "What's the big hurry? We were having fun hop-scotching on the bone piles," he said with a wink.

"Psycho cat found me while I was looking for animals in the clouds. She rubbed against me and purred. She even let me skritch her behind the ears and was really quite friendly," Molly explained.

"Are you nuts? You're lucky that you didn't get your

face ripped off. Don't you remember how she beat up that seagull?" cried Adam.

"No," said Molly, "I think the cat might be Great Grandma Ruby, and she wants us to follow her so come on, hurry up," she continued.

The boys looked at Molly with hesitancy, sharing the same thought that she may be crazy after all. They decided to trust her though and followed the cat up the beach to the entrance of the other cave. Psycho cat wound the children along the narrow passage to the opening where they had seen the light shining on the wet walls. Adam realized that the opening looked out on the cove where the boat was drawn. The cat kept looking up to one corner of the cave and meowing.

"Look, there is something up there that is shining," said Gord. "Adam, give me a boost so I can get a closer look."

Adam got down on all fours while Gord climbed upon his back. Carefully, he reached up and found a silver wedding band hanging on a nail. Gord removed it and said, "It looks like something is engraved on the inside. I can't make out what it is because it is so tarnished."

"Let's take it home and see if we can find some silver polish," suggested Molly. "Maybe this is a clue to help us with the mystery".

It was time to get back to the farm for supper, as the adults wanted to leave early to go to the square dance. The sun was still shining brightly and there was not a cloud in the sky. Adam looked up and surveyed the sky.

"Tonight is going to be crystal clear without a cloud in sight..., a perfect night to view the Phantom Ship," he said in his best weather man voice.

CHAPTER 21

The Square Dance

Supper was quick and delicious consisting of Aunt Ann's famous spaghetti and meat balls with large slices of fresh garlic bread. Mom, Aunt Ann, and Uncle Rob put on their fancy duds and were just about to head out the door when Mom said "We will phone around nine o'clock, just to make sure that everything is all right."

"You don't have to do that Mom. Seriously, we are not babies you know," scolded Gord, since he was left in charge.

"I would just be more comfortable knowing that everything is good and that you are getting ready for bed. Aunt Ann left some cinnamon buns with cream cheese frosting that you like so much for a bedtime snack. I'll call at 9," replied Mom.

"If you say so. I will make sure we all get to bed on time. Now get out of here and enjoy the dance," Gord replied.

"Well I guess it is settled, we can't go down to the beach until after we get the call," said Adam with an air of disappointment in his voice.

"Let's get some silver polish and see if we can find out what is engraved in the ring," said Molly.

They found some silver polish under the sink and with an old piece of cloth Adam scrubbed at the ring until all of the tarnish was gone. Inscribed on the inside of the ring were the letters R and B with the date Aug. 5.

"Ruby and Ben," said Molly.

"They must have been married on the fifth of August." stated Gord.

"I'm really quite sure that Psycho Cat is Great Grandma Ruby. Why else would she lead us to the ring?" questioned Molly.

"She must want us to have the ring, or perhaps it is another clue to help us in our search for the Phantom Ship," answered Adam.

"This must have been Grandfather Ben's ring," Gord rationalized

"Look how big it is, I bet it is the same size as the skull ring that we found. Maybe we should check it out," said Adam.

Gord pulled out the skull ring and put it next to the wedding band and stated," A perfect match."

"It must be his. But why was it placed on that nail? What happened out there?" Molly questioned.

The kids decided to look through the family album to see if they could find any more clues. It was only eight o'clock and they knew that they had at least another hour before mom would call.

"Be very careful with the album, we don't want to tear any of the old pictures," Molly said as she watched her brother turn the pages slowly. There were pictures of Ben in his army uniform and of Ruby in the garden, and there was also the 'Psycho cat' beside her in three of the pictures.

CHAPTER 22

The Call Came and so Did the Boat

Just then the phone rang and they all jumped. Adam looked at the clock and said "8:30, she's calling early. Hurry and pick it up so we can get out of here." After a short minute Gord assured Mom that everything was good and they were getting ready for bed soon. He hung up the phone and announced "It's all clear. Now let's get ready to go down to the beach."

The kids packed the cinnamon buns that were supposed to be for a bedtime snack, a jug of juice, warm clothes, flashlights, a pocket knife, Uncle Rob's binoculars, the spyglass that they found in the trunk, and a sleeping bag in case it got really cold. The three then set out down the driveway to the gate and towards the rocks at the beach. As Adam had predicted earlier, it was a calm and quiet night without a cloud in the sky. The moon sat just above the water and shone as bright as a beacon across the water, while casting a light along the path they travelled. A lone seagull hovered overhead in search of food scraps or a careless minnow venturing too close to the surface of the water.

"I wonder if that is what people are mistaking for the Phantom Ship," suggested Molly.

"Don't be crazy Molly, we saw the Phantom Ship the other night and that was no moon," scolded Gord.

They walked along the waters edge not needing their flashlights as the moon and thousands of stars lit up the sky. Continuing up the beach to the cove, the children found a nice little nook in the rocks, set down a blanket and spread out their bedtime snack. Now all they had to do was wait and see if anything would happen on this clear evening. The kids sat and talked mostly about what they had found and how most of it pointed to Great Grandma Ruby and Great Grandpa Ben. They wondered if the pirates had captured Ben and stole his rings, wooden eye, eye patch and the Ruby's Hands pendant. They also wondered what it would have been like to live in their time where the world seemed to be a different place. Several thoughts crossed the minds of the clever little children but the one that remained through all of the questions and discussions was that of the phantom ship.

"Maybe Old Ben was a pirate," chuckled Gord.

"I told you to never say that again," groaned Molly. "He would never do something like that.

Besides, Molly knew differently, for she had talked with Old Ben that night on the foot of her bed. She thought that this might be a good time to tell the boys about her conversation, but then thought that they might think she was crazy.

Gord took out the binoculars and surveyed the bay.

There seemed to be a rowboat floating in the distance in their direction. There did not seem to be anyone in it however. It was at the mercy of the tide and it seemed to be following the shoreline. Soon Gord could not see it any more as it disappeared around the edge of the cove.

"Someone must have forgotten to tie their rowboat up or put the anchor down," he exclaimed.

Off in the distance there was a light glowing, just on the edge of the horizon. As they watched with enthusiasm, the light grew with intensity and there was no doubt that it was indeed the Phantom Ship, again. Gord picked up the spy glass and looked towards the light.

"This must be broken. It is not magnifying anything," said Gord. "Maybe it's just an ordinary glass." He grabbed the binoculars and looked through them at the light, and then at a tree and back to the light. He did this three times to make sure that his observations were right.

"These binoculars make the tree bigger but not the light, what's up with that?" Gord inquired with an ere of puzzlement in his voice.

"Here, let me take a look," said Adam as he tested both the spyglass and the binoculars. "That's just weird," he said as he put the glasses down and gazed out on the bay.

The light was growing in intensity and a fiery outline of a ship with three distinct masts was rising from the surface of the bay. The masts were a blaze and as the ship rose from the water, the light continued to get brighter. Spark-like fireballs started to explode from the boat into the air and faint screams began to intensify in sound and pitch. The children looked at each other with an eerie and slightly frightful expression as they continued to watch the burning ship.

"Wow, you can see it so much better from here than the other night," said Gord.

Just then, Molly looked over to the edge of the cove. The moon had gone behind a cloud and a beam of light was shining through a hole in the clouds. It was shining right down onto the rowboat that they had seen earlier. Only now, it was on the edge of the beach and it looked like a spot light was shining directly on it.

"Look guys, the rowboat is on the shore," exclaimed Molly.

"Maybe we could get in it and row out to the Phantom Ship," suggested Gord.

"I don't know, we don't have life jackets and we are not strong swimmers," Molly said.

"If we stay close to the shore where it isn't too deep than we should be O.K." suggested Adam with a hint of concern.

"I don't care about life jackets, I'm going to row out there," said Gord with a stern voice. "Who's coming with me?"

Gord was strong willed and both Adam and Molly knew that no matter what they said to him or how risky a voyage this might be, that he was still going to go. Adam and Molly agreed that there was safety in numbers, and they decided to go with Gord as long as they could shine their flashlight on the water and see what was lurking below.

The three children climbed hesitantly into the rowboat which surprisingly seemed to be quite large and sturdy. Adam and Gord took an oar and Molly sat up front with her flashlight. The boys started to row and Molly shone her light on the bottom of the bay to make sure they were staying in the shallow water. As the boys rowed towards the Phantom Ship they could hear the screams getting louder and more frightening. The fire balls were glowing and falling into the water from all areas of the ship's masts. They rowed in the direction of the burning ship, but they didn't seem to be making any headway. No matter how hard Adam and Gord rowed they didn't seem to be getting any closer to the Phantom Ship.

"Come on guys, can't you row any faster than that? It's getting away." shouted Molly.

"We are rowing as fast as we can, but we are not getting any closer to the boat." replied Gord. What the heck is going on?" he queried.

"I wish we could get closer to the ship and see what is engulfed in flames and falling into the water. I also want to know what is making those ghastly screams," said Adam.

The boys tried rowing faster to no avail. The Phantom Ship continued to burn, the flaming balls of fire continued to fall, the screams continued to echo across the otherwise calm surface of the water and the children were beginning to feel exhausted. It all seemed weird, crazy and scary.

"The strange thing about this whole experience is that the fire isn't sputtering out as it hits the water," thought Adam.

Then as the children continued to watch the burning boat, the fire balls lessened and the eerie screams began to fade. The Phantom Ship's flames were not as intense anymore and gradually it sank beneath the surface of the water, as if it had never been there to begin with.

"No matter how hard we rowed we couldn't get any closer to it. There was no heat generated from the fire. It's all, very strange and frighteningly weird," sighed Gord.

"It just seems like we are watching a movie," replied Molly.

Molly suddenly realized that they were in deep water and she couldn't see the bottom any more. In the excitement and rowing towards the Phantom Ship she had forgotten to keep watch on the bottom.

"Guys, let's get back to the beach before this boat tips over and we all drown, or worse, become part of the Phantom Ship," she continued with a tremble in her voice.

Gord and Adam slowly turned the boat around and headed towards the shore and within minutes, were pulling the rowboat up onto the safety of the beach.

The children decided that they should get back to the farmhouse as it was fast approaching midnight and the adults would be returning home soon.

Just as the children were opening the back door of the house, they saw the truck lights coming up the driveway. They quickly dove into their beds and pretended to be asleep when Mom came in to check on them.

"That old boat sure came in handy. What an adventure!" thought Gord, as he lay in bed relaying the events of the night.

CHAPTER 23

What the Grown Up's Saw

I n the morning, the kids all slept in. Molly was the first to awaken and sleepily walked into the kitchen where Mom was having a hot cup of tea.

"You sure had a good sleep," Mom said to Molly.

"We went to bed a bit late last night. They boys and I were playing board games and time got away from us," Molly responded with a yawn.

This was the story that she and the boys had agreed on if asked what they got up to the night before. Molly felt a little guilty because she didn't like lying to her Mom. A hug from Mom and an "I missed you last night," made it all right however.

"How was the dance anyway?" Molly asked.

"Oh, it was just fine. We boogied and line danced,

dipped and twirled." Mom replied. "We are all a bit tired today too," she continued.

About an hour later, coming on 11:30am, Gord and Adam came up the stairs.

"So who won all the games last night?" Mom asked.

"Aaaah, we each won some," answered Adam. It took him a few seconds to get his story straight as he was still half asleep.

Gord and Adam went out to help with the few remaining chores and Molly went to her room, sat by the window and read her book. It was <u>Ann of Green Gables</u> and she could relate to Ann's imagination which was not unlike hers.

The heater vent was below Molly's window and she could hear Aunt Ann and Mom talking about their night out and how they too, had seen the Phantom Ship. Mom and Aunt Ann discussed how strange it seemed as they watched from the lawn of the hall.

Molly could not believe what she was hearing and put her book down beside her bed. She put her ear real close to the vent to make sure what she was hearing was true.

Aunt Ann said "Wasn't it so strange that the rowboat moving towards the ship, had paddled right through it while it was still a blaze? How did it not catch fire?"

"For my first encounter with the Phantom Ship, I still feel very uneasy about what we saw. I struggled to sleep last night from both the mysteriousness of the ship, and fright about the screams we heard. I'm not sure I will ever get them out of my head," Mom responded quietly.

"There are so many bad things that are associated with that horrible Phantom Ship," said Aunt Ann. "I'm sure the devil has something to do with it."

"I have heard of the Phantom Ship before, but actually seeing it for myself made me feel scared and confused."

This conversation scared Molly because this was the first time that she heard Aunt Ann admit that she knew anything about the Phantom Ship. Molly put her book back on the bed and ran out to the barn to tell Gord and Adam about the conversation that she had overheard. She waited patiently until Uncle Rob was out of ear shot to tell the boys. She was almost vibrating with excitement as she tried to relay the whole story without missing a thing.

"Are you kidding me, they saw our rowboat go right through the Phantom Ship?" exclaimed Adam.

"I really don't understand what is happening with this strange Phantom Ship. Where does it come from and why couldn't we get close to it?" questioned Gord.

"This is all so strange, very strange," replied Molly.

"Why don't we sneak out again tonight and see if we can find any more clues that would lead us closer to solving the mystery of the Phantom Ship?" Gord suggested.

Molly decided to take a pass as she was really tired from all the activities of the previous night and did not want to admit that she was both overwhelmed and frightened by what they had seen. At supper that night Gord thought that he would try and get a little information from Mom and Aunt Ann of what they had seen the night before.

"Hey Mom, did you have fun at the dance last night? Anything interesting happen that you would like to tell us about?" Gord questioned.

Mom looked at Aunt Ann and neither one of them said anything for a short while. Then Mom felt that some sort of response was necessary so she replied "We had lots of fun square dancing and seeing people that I had gone to school with. I hadn't seen for quite a few years. We danced the night away, reminisced about old times, and shared stories of our current lives."

It was pretty obvious to the children that they were not about to talk about seeing the Phantom Ship, so Gord dropped the subject.

Adam was not about to give up though and thought that he would give it a try.

"I woke up last night and came up to get a drink of the water. I saw a flaming light on the bay. It looked a bit like a boat. What do you suppose it could have been?"

Uncle Rob looked at Aunt Ann and Mom, with a disturbed look across his face as if he were deep in thought. It appeared to the children that he was trying to come up with an explanation that was both plausible and realistic.

"It could have been a bonfire on the beach and the reflections were shining on the water," Uncle Rob suggested.

"It looked bigger than a bonfire but it was late… Maybe you are right Uncle Rob." Adam replied while thinking to himself. "What was this Phantom Ship and why won't anyone talk about it?"

CHAPTER 24

The Extra Passenger

The boys went downstairs to get read for bed early than usual. They wanted a chance to look over their box of treasures again, and the map they had found, to see if they could have missed something along the way.

Suddenly it dawned on Adam. "Gord, the rowboat that was in the cove could have been what was marked on the map!"

"How could that be though?" asked Gord "The rowboat wasn't there before."

"This is very, very strange," Adam said in his best detective voice.

Molly had gone to bed early too, and was sleeping soundly long before Mom, Uncle Rob and Aunt Ann decided to turn in. When Gord and Adam felt that everyone was asleep they quietly snuck out the bedroom window, being careful not to make a noise. With a backpack stocked full of their map and treasures, a few snacks, a blanket, and a flashlight, the boys climbed down the rocks to the beach and headed straight for the cove. They looked along the shore of the beach but the rowboat was nowhere to be seen. They looked quizzically at each other and continued to search for something or anything out of the ordinary.

"Maybe whoever owns that rowboat came by and took it back to wherever they live," said Gord.

The boys retreated back to the first cave as it looked like there might be a chance of rain. All was quiet except for an occasional rustle of leaves in the gusting winds. The waves took turns rushing up the sand at the waters edge only to retreat into the rippling waters of the bay. The boys shivered as they sat in the cave but they would not dare let the wind send them home before they uncovered the mystery.

"Nothing much happening so far," said Gord.

"Aaaaaah der be nothin' right now, maybe she will come soon, no?" said Adam in his best French accent. They both laughed and shook their heads.

"Waiting can be so boring," Gord yawned.

It seemed like they had been waiting for hours, sharing jokes, passing the time, and snacking on some trail mix when suddenly – a spark, a light, a beacon of some sort slowly started to rise out of the bay. It was barely visible and for all the boys knew, it could be a star on the horizon.

But no! This was not a star. The light grew with intensity and changed from a whitish yellow colour to an overwhelmingly bright orange, as it seemed to approach the shore. Adam jumped up and started to run down the beach.

"Come on Gord, let's go down by the cove for a better look," he shouted over his shoulder. They ran as fast as their legs would carry them until Adam grabbed Gord by the arm and said, "Gord, Stop! Look! There is that light shining down through the hole in the cloud again."

At the end of the light, there it was again – the rowboat. This time there was a passenger. The black cat was sitting on the front of the boat peering out to sea. She sat there as though she too, had a mission to accomplish.

"I thought cats hate water," said Adam.

"Maybe that is why she is in the boat, smarty pants," chuckled Gord.

This seemed like too much of a coincidence, that the same rowboat at the end of the same moonbeam, sat awaiting their arrival. The boys were wondering what was going on and why Psycho Cat was sitting in the boat this time?

"Should we get in the boat with Psycho Cat? If she decides to attack us there is nowhere to go except in the water and you and I both know that we are NOT good swimmers." stated Gord.

"This all seems too good to be true but we haven't come this far, to turn away because of a little black cat. After all, Molly did say she was becoming friendlier. Someone, somewhere, wants us to get in this boat. I think Psycho Cat will guide us to the mystery of the Phantom Ship," Adam replied confidently

"If the cat attacks, I will knock her into the drink with my oar," said Gord.

Very, very carefully, Adam and Gord climbed into the boat with the cat as their guide. The cat just looked at them and meowed quietly as she looked out towards the Phantom Ship. It continued to grow in intensity as moved slowly across the water and closer to them. The boys started to row towards the burning light. Now the faint screams they were hearing, started to sound as though the people making the noise were in the row boat with the boys. They were almost piercing, and for a moment, the boys covered their ears and shuddered.

As the rowboat continued in the direction of the fiery light Adam said, "Look, you can see the three masts on the ship and fire balls that are starting to explode!"

The boys continued to row towards the Phantom Ship and just as the previous time they got to a place where forward progress stopped, no matter how hard they rowed. Suddenly the cat turned and meowed rather loudly (not your everyday meow) and sounded like she was saying, "rrrrright."

"Maybe she is telling us to turn right," said Adam.

"Just row on your side and that will make us turn right," Gord said.

The boat started to move again as soon as Adam started to row. They weren't getting any closer but they were moving parallel to the burning beacon and could see the shape of the fiery ship. As they moved along the water, the fire was burning fiercely. Now the sounds of eerie screams echoed in their ears, and all of the tiny hairs stood up on the back of Gord's neck. No matter what they did or how hard they rowed, they could not get any closer. They just kept moving parallel to the Phantom Ship. It was as if there was an invisible wall, a force to be reckoned with, that prevented them from approaching the Phantom Ship. Gord guesstimated that they were about fifty feet away.

"If those are real flames we would feel the heat and there would be the sound of fizzling. Fire can't burn in water," said Gord.

Adam was busily scanning the horizon for clues and Psycho Cat was becoming agitated. She was pacing back and forth along the seat at the front of the boat.

"What's up with the cat?" asked Adam.

Just then a scream and a flutter of wings disturbed the

silence and Adam almost fell out of the boat. Gord grabbed him by the jacket and pulled him back onto his seat.

"What the H – E – double hockey sticks was that?" cried Adam. His mother did not like the boys cursing and this was what Adam always said instead of getting Mom upset, while at the same time feeling that he got away with saying a bad word.

They looked up high into the sky and saw a huge black bird of some kind flying over and circling the top of the Phantom Ship. It was making strange and disturbing noises, almost as if it was yelling obscenities at something or someone.

"I bet that's Old Ben, but what do you suppose he is doing or saying?" questioned Gord.

As they watched the big bird circling and screaming God only knows what, at the Phantom Ship, the burning ship started to lose the intensity and the fireballs coming from the ship ceased flying. The screams stopped and the ship slowly slipped beneath the surface of the water. In no time at all, everything became calm and peaceful as if nothing had ever happened.

The big black bird seemed to vanish in thin air. All this time the two boys' eyes were riveted on what was happening. They looked at each other and to the front of the boat.

"Hey, where did Psycho Cat go?" asked Gord.

"We didn't hear her jump into the water, cats hate water," replied Adam.

They looked all around in every direction. She was nowhere to be found.

"This is freakin' weird, nothing here makes sense," said Gord.

Carefully, the boys rowed out to where the burning ship looked to have been. There was nothing to suggest that a ship or anything else, as a matter of fact, had been on fire there. No burned wood, no ashes, no evidence of any kind that what they witnessed just moments ago, had even happened... and where the heck did Psycho Cat go? These were all questions that did not appear to have any answers. They also wondered why they were able to paddle across the lake, now that the boat had vanished.

"Let's go back to Uncle Rob's and come back during the day tomorrow. Maybe there are more clues in the caves that we missed," said Adam.

They rowed the boat ashore and tied it to a large piece of driftwood. The walk back to the farmhouse seemed a lot longer tonight. The boys were lost in their own thoughts and made their way back distractedly. Little did they know, trouble was brewing. Mom had woken up to go to the bathroom about fifteen minutes earlier and went downstairs to look in on the boys and discovered that they were not there. She had awoken Uncle Rob and Aunt Ann and was about ready to call the police when Molly heard the commotion and came out of her room.

"Do you know where the boys are Molly?" questioned her Mother in a very worried voice. Before Molly could answer the boys burst through the door and Adam said "Hey, why is everyone up, did we miss a party or something?"

"Where were you? You had us worried sick, we were about to call the police," queried Mom with a tone full of fear and disappointment.

"Uhhhhh, I got up to go to the bathroom about an hour ago and saw that strange light on the bay so I woke Gord. We walked down to the beach for a better look. I'm sorry we worried you, we thought that you were asleep, right Gord?"

Gord was silent and then said, "Yeah, that's why we were

gone, I guess we didn't realise that someone would wake up and worry, we are so sorry, aren't we Adam?"

"Sorry or not, you boys should not have just left like that. You have no idea how worried I was. We will talk about a punishment in the morning," Mom replied sternly.

"I'd really like to know where that strange fiery light is coming from. Do any of you know?" asked Adam.

Again there was a long uncomfortable silence until Aunt Ann cleared her throat and very quietly said, "Don't go sticking your nose where it doesn't belong. Curiosity killed the cat you know. You stay away from that beach at night, and that is my last word. Now let's all go back to bed."

Mom went up with Molly and tucked her into bed. She had trouble sleeping because she knew that Adam and Gord would have an adventure to tell her about in the morning.

Aunt Ann watched as Adam and Gord sheepishly slunk down the stairs into the toy room. They looked back and gave her a smile, but they both knew that they were in mounds of trouble. Not a word was said, while they both crawled under their covers and closed their eyes.

CHAPTER 25

What Would I Be?

Molly had thoughts about Psycho Cat and the crow that she affectionately referred to as Ruby and Old Ben, and from that point on, she had decided that is what the children would call the animals. She peered out the window and watched the dark clouds playing tag with the moon. Molly had a way of making the best of every situation and her wonderful imagination sometimes added life to an otherwise ordinary scene.

She thought that she liked the idea of reincarnation and was happy to know her great grandparents, even if they were not in the bodies of real people. She felt a warm comfortable feeling envelope her body as she wondered what she could come back as. A dove, a cute little bunny, or maybe a cuddly kitten, so she could hang out with Ruby. Molly continued to let the warm thoughts swirl around in her brain until she slowly drifted of to sleep.

The next morning the boys brought Molly up to speed about the extra passenger the night before and what had happened. She was amazed that Ruby had gone along for the ride.

"Where do you suppose Ruby disappeared to?" asked Molly.

"Who knows? That cat seems to possess some special kind of magical powers. Maybe she was with us all the time and just turned invisible," Gord sad wonderingly.

"I never thought that turning invisible was an option," responded Adam.

"I wonder if the Phantom Ship is a bunch of bad pirates who are doomed to live this horrible experience over and over again," pondered Molly aloud.

"Uncle Rob did say that some people believe that what you come back as, is determined by how you lived your life," said Adam.

"If they were bad, mean pirates, why wouldn't they come back as snakes or rats or something that is creepy and ugly?" Gord reasoned.

"Maybe they were so mean that God decided that even Hell was too good for them and they had no place to go," said Molly.

"Neither Heaven or Hell wants them so they are destined to relive their horror over and over again!" exclaimed Adam in his best Ghost story voice.

CHAPTER 26

Ruby Returns

"**L**et's go down to the beach and search the caves again. Maybe we missed something that will help us figure out this whole mess anyway," said Gord.

Gord asked Mom if they could go down to the beach to gather some seashells for a picture they were planning to give to Aunt Ann. He knew if he said they were going exploring after sneaking out the night before, that mom would surely say no.

"You boys are still in trouble after sneaking out last night. You'd better not be looking for that silly boat! A picture for Aunt Ann does sound nice though. I guess it is O.K. so long as you are back in time for supper. We are all invited over to my friend Martha's for dessert later this evening," said Mom.

The children assured her that they would be back in

time for supper and set off towards the beach. When they arrived at the beach Gord and Adam wanted to explore the cave with the bones first. Molly decided to stay on the beach and make a sand castle as those stinkin' bones gave her the creeps. She also decided to look for some pretty shells so she could make Aunt Ann a nice picture. It seemed like the right thing to do after giving her such a fright.

Gord warned Molly not to go exploring on her own because who knows what danger lurked around the next corner. Molly assured Gord that she would be right where she was now when they came back from the cave, but not to be too long.

Gord and Adam explored the entrance. Nothing seemed different so they climbed up on the ledge and gently let themselves down on the floor of the inner cave, taking care not to step on the bones this time.

A bat flew over Gord's head causing him to jump out of the way. He landed on some more bones and let out a yell as he shivered and took a quick step to the left, just to trip over a round metal rod sticking out of the ground.

"These bones just creep me out," said Gord as a shiver went down his back. He looked down to see what he had tripped over and saw the metal rod amongst the creepy bones. He grabbed it with both hands and pulled. Nothing happened. He stood back and gave it a good hard kick. It loosened a bit and as he reached down to pull it out, he saw what looked to be, the bottom of a rather large key.

"What do you suppose this will open?" questioned Gord.

The boys had only been in the cave for a few minutes when Molly felt something rub up against her back. At first it took her by surprise and Molly looked all around her. You can imagine her surprise when she realized that it was just the cat. Ruby rubbed her head up against Molly's shoulder and started to purr.

"Hi Ruby" Molly said softly as she began to scratch Ruby behind her ear. The cat purred and closed her eyes as her back arched and stretched, as if this was the first affection that was shown to her in a very long time. After a few minutes of thoroughly enjoying the undivided attention of this charming little girl, Ruby stretched and walked about five or six feet away. She looked right at Molly and meowed but to Molly's disbelief, it sounded more like "come on." Ruby started walking up the beach.

Molly did not know what to do since she had told the boys that she would wait right there beside the entrance to the cave. Then again, Ruby wanted Molly to follow her. Decisions, decisions… what was she to do? Molly knew that Gord would be upset and worried if he came out and discovered her missing.

"Ruby, where do you want me to go?" she asked. Ruby came back and rubbed up against Molly's leg and once again repeated the meow that sounded even more like "come on". Molly decided that she would follow Ruby as far as she could as long as the boys could see her from the entrance to the cave.

Molly followed the cat to the entrance of the cave where the boys had gone in only moments ago.

Molly looked at Ruby and said, "I'm not going in there." The cat wandered back to where Molly was standing and rubbed her back up against Molly's leg once again. She then gave that familiar meow that again sounded like "come on." Molly paused for a moment, then reached down and scratched Ruby's ears.

"O.K., I'll come with you if that's what you really want Ruby," said Molly.

Molly followed the cat to a group of rocks that was about

fifty feet from the cave entrance. She had not noticed before, but there was a rock that was shaped like a crow's head, so long as you let your imagination run wild.

The cat pawed at the stone as if she was trying to move them.

"What are you doing? What's under those rocks?" asked Molly.

Ruby was not making much headway so Molly decided to help her. She carefully lifted some of the smaller rocks and moved them aside. Molly had moved about half a dozen rocks when she saw Adam and Gord coming out of the cave.

"Find anything interesting boys?" asked Molly.

"Not really" said Gord "Except for this bottom of a large old key."

"What are you doing Molly?" asked Adam.

"Ruby told me to come on with her meowing, and led me here," she said. "She was trying to move these rocks. Come on and help me move some more rocks," she continued.

The boys helped and soon all the rocks were moved. There was nothing underneath.

"What gives? There is nothing under these rocks," said Gord.

The cat jumped into the spot and furiously started digging with her front paws. Sand was flying everywhere.

"Here, let us help you Ruby," exclaimed Molly as she and the boys started to dig with their hands.

"Wait, look there! What is that sticking out of the ground?" shouted Adam.

More digging revealed a shaft with a crow's head on it made out of brass.

"Wait a minute, this looks like it could be the top half of our key. Give me that other piece Gord," said Adam .Very carefully, he fit the two pieces together and they instantly bonded and the key started to glow and give off an eerie bright blue light. Adam instantly dropped the key and jumped back.

"Whoa," he shrieked. "What the heck is that?" The three kids watched in amazement as the blue light turned to red and then to yellow and slowly went back to its original brass colour.

"That is the strangest thing that I have ever seen," said Molly.

"Even stranger than the Phantom Ship?" questioned Adam.

"Well maybe not, but I have never seen a key do that before." Gord bent over to pick it up and examine it more thoroughly.

"Be careful, it still might be hot!" exclaimed Adam.

Gord picked it up and studied it for clues. It was a very large key, like nothing that he had seen before. It was about a foot and a half long and the shaft was as thick as a broomstick.

"What kind of a lock could this key be used to open?" Gord inquired.

After examining it for another minute he concluded that it must have magical powers because why else would it glow like it did? In all the commotion no one saw Ruby leave.

"She just disappears whenever she wants, remember in the boat when she seemed to vanish," said Gord. "I feel sure, that this is a very important clue. It is the most magical of any of the things that that we have, found other than the Phantom Ship itself."

The kids walked back towards the farm, all the time trying to think of what the key would possibly open – A really big treasure chest, a huge door leading to who knows where, a really big safe? These were some of the ideas that were discussed.

"I don't think this magical key with the crows head opens any doors at all," said Molly. "I think Old Ben probably knows what it's about. Has anyone seen him lately?"

"We haven't seen him since the last sighting of the Phantom Ship when he was flying over the ship and yelling things at it," worried Adam.

CHAPTER 27

The Headless Chicken

"I think we should sneak out tonight and bring the key. I'm sure it has something to do with unlocking the mystery of the Phantom Ship," suggested Adam.

"We can't go out tonight, Mom expects us to go over to her friend Martha's tonight, remember," reminded Molly.

"Oh darn, maybe we can get out of going, or come down here much later." said Gord.

The children arrived back at the farm a little while before supper and decided to see if Uncle Rob needed help with the afternoon chores. Uncle Rob was out at the hen pen selecting a nice fat hen for tomorrow night's dinner.

"You can stay and help pluck this chicken after I kill it," said Uncle Rob, after the boys asked what could be done.

"Eeewww, gross," shouted Molly, as she ran back to the

house. Gord and Adam decided to stay as this would be a new experience.

"Are you sure you want to watch me kill this chicken? I use an axe and cut its head off you know," said Uncle Rob.

"I'm staying, I think this might be interesting," responded Gord.

Uncle Rob grabbed a hen by the legs, put the head down on a wooden block and with one swipe of the axe cut the head off clean and put the chicken on the ground. It ran around for a couple of seconds before it fell lifeless to the dirt.

"Wow, I guess that is where the expression "Running around like a chicken with its head cut off comes from." thought Gord aloud.

Uncle Rob showed the boys how to pluck and clean the chicken and then they headed into the farmhouse to wash up for supper. Aunt Ann had a nice roast beef stew with big fluffy dumplings waiting for them.

"So, did you collect some nice shells or find anything else interesting at the beach?" Mom asked the kids. They all looked at each other knowingly, and Molly said, "Oh, same old, same old. We picked up a few pretty shells that we will show you later."

"Mom, do we really have to go to your friend Martha's tonight?" asked Adam. Mom paused for a minute and replied, "Well, it probably will be pretty boring for you and if you want, you can stay home and play games again. Uncle Rob, Aunt Ann and I will probably play cards for awhile and will be back around 10:30."

"You don't have to phone tonight and check up on us, we're not babies you know?" said Gord.

"O.K., I won't phone you, but don't get into any trouble. Molly's bedtime is 8:30 tonight alright? She's been really sleepy the last few days."

Molly protested a bit to play along and then helped Aunt Ann with the dishes. The grownups got dressed, climbed into the old pickup truck and headed out to Martha's place.

CHAPTER 28

The Magical Key

"O.K. guys let's head for the beach and this time we better bring the key," said Adam. Gord looked puzzled while lines formed across his forehead.

"Where is that map? I want to see something." asked Gord.

Adam got the map and handed it to him. After looking at the map for a minute, Gord let out a gasp.

"Look up here in the left hand corner, there is a tiny key hole with flames around it. How come we never noticed it before? What could this possibly mean? Is this yet another clue?"

The kids started to walk to the beach and Adam suggested that they start their search at the cove.

"I wonder if that rowboat is still there?" pondered Molly. "Without it, how will we get to the key hole?"

When the children arrived at the cove it was still dusk and there was no sign of the boat. They sat down on a large log and waited patiently for darkness to fall. All this time, Adam was studying the magical key. He kept turning the key over and over in his hands searching for something, possibly a clue, a hint, something to give them direction.

"I'm stumped, but I feel almost positive that this key will unlock the mystery of the Phantom Ship," said Adam.

For the next few minutes they talked about all the things that they had found. Most of the objects that they had found seemed to involve their great grandparents Ben and Ruby. How could they possibly be tied to the mystery of the Phantom Ship? Had they been captured by pirates or was there the possibility that they were pirates? There were so many pieces to the puzzle and not much time to put them all together. Their vacation was nearly over and the children really wanted to solve the mystery before they had to go back to school.

By now it was starting to get dark and all eyes were on the horizon in watch for the Phantom Ship.

"How can we get closer to the ship if we have no boat?" questioned Gord.

"Look over there! I think I can see a spark on the water!" shouted Molly.

Sure enough, that familiar beacon that they had seen on previous occasions was rising out of the surface of the water. Slowly and steadily the beacon burned as the flames took the shape of the Phantom Ship.

"Hey boys, over there," said Molly as she pointed to the beam of light shining down on the rowboat, sitting just a few feet from the shore.

"Come on you guys, let's go before the Phantom Ship slips beneath the surface of the water again," said Gord.

They ran as fast as they possibly could with Gord reaching the water first, splashing to grab hold of the rope before it drifted away. "Quick guys get in," Gord continued, as he held it steady while Adam and Molly climbed aboard.

Soon they took their familiar positions in the boat with Molly upfront watching the depth of the water, and Gord and Adam manning the oars. They rowed with all their might and the rowboat slid over the top of the water. Within moments, they reached the area that seemed to impede their progress as both boys rowed fearlessly through the calmness of the water.

"We are not making any headway but remember what the cat said... 'Rrrrright'," Adam said as he mimicked the cat's meow from the previous encounter. They moved to the right and drifted parallel to the glowing lights that were now cascading off the ship. The faint scream like noises echoed across the bay and like each encounter before, the flames got brighter and then disappeared into the surface of the water.

"Man, there is definitely something strange. I can't figure out why the lights or fireballs or whatever the H – E – double hockey sticks, those things are, don't fizzle like a match when it hits the water," said Adam.

"The flames, or light, or whatever it is, doesn't seem real. It's like we are in a scene from a really scary movie or something!" Molly cried.

"Tonight, the Phantom Ship is amazing to see. The three masts are very recognisable even though the complete ship is engulfed in flames," Adam said using his best announcer voice. "And," he continued with hi Frankenstein impression, "No one seems to know what the fireballs are. Some suspect that these ghosts are not really ghosts, that they are souls that neither God nor the Devil wanted and they have been sentenced to forever live their fiery deaths over and over and over."

"Stop that, you are scaring me," wept Molly as she slapped Adam's shoulder and pouted with her bottom lip turned out.

The night was very dark, the sky was covered with clouds, and there was only a sliver of the moon that was partially hidden by a bird shaped cloud. The reflection of the Phantom Ship cascaded out across the water to almost where the rowboat was as the three children watched in awe.

CHAPTER 29

The Flaming Keyhole

The flap of wings could be heard from above and a large bird like shadow soared across the shimmering waters.

"It must be Old Ben!" shrieked Molly. The big bird seemed to be carrying something shiny, something glowing. Suddenly he dropped it and it was falling towards the surface of the water not more than twenty feet from their rowboat. The shiny object was to the right of them and just before it hit the water it seemed to stop and hover a just a foot above the surface.

"What do you suppose that is? A giant firefly?" asked Molly.

"That's no firefly," responded Gord.

"Come on Gord, let's keep rowing," encouraged Adam.

As they got closer to the glowing object, it started to take the shape of a rather large lock surrounded by flames. The kids looked upon the flaming lock with awe and paddled as fast as their arms allowed, panting with each strong stride.

"It's the flaming keyhole from the map!" exclaimed Gord. They looked towards the Phantom Ship and discovered that it was slowly sinking below the surface of the bay as the cascade of light rolled back to meet the ship while it disappeared beneath the water's surface. The eerie screams also faded but this time they seemed to echo a spine chilling effect as they faded away to nothing.

A few more strokes of the oars and they were within arm's reach of the flaming keyhole.

"Pass me the magical key Adam," said Gord. "The flaming Phantom Ship, the flaming lock, maybe this magical key unlocks the mystery to the Phantom Ship!" he exclaimed, with much excitement in his voice.

"Be careful that you don't fall in Gord," cautioned Molly "You don't swim well," she continued. Gord and Molly carefully switched places while Adam rowed the boat a little closer so that Gord could reach the keyhole.

"Be careful that you don't burn yourself," warned Molly. She was always concerned that someone would get hurt.

"I couldn't burn myself even if I tried," said Gord. "There is no heat coming from the flames. Look I can wave my hand right through it and it does not burn me in the slightest," he continued as he demonstrated the feat of courage.

Then slowly and carefully he inserted the magical crow headed key into the flaming keyhole. Nothing happened.

"Turn the key in the lock," said Adam quietly.

Slowly, but steadily, Gord turned the key to the left, nothing happened. Then he heard a cat call in his mind, the same one he had heard when Ruby was in the boat.

"Rrrrrright", she purred, and Gord turned the key to the right.

Within seconds, a large blinding white light engulfed the row boat. They were floating in some misty fog covered waters with the sun shining down upon a large three masted ship only a short distance away. There were faint sounds that were the voices of many rowdy drunken men, and the bright lights on deck were almost too much to bare.

"Where are we? What is this? Is that the Phantom Ship? How come it is not burning?" asked Molly in a very frightened voice.

Adam looked at the key and at the ship and then back at the key again. He concluded that the mysterious magical key possessed powers of time travel and it had carried them back in time to before the pirate ship had caught fire.

"This is so amazing but also a little bit scary," said Adam aloud.

"No, make that a lot scary. Those mean pirates are going to capture us and we will never get back to the farm or see Mom again!" wept Molly.

"Don't be afraid Molly everything is going to be all right, God will take care of us," said Gord in a reassuring voice as he put his arm around her. He did not seem so confident, but he figured that this might help Molly to be less worried and to stop crying.

Just then, Gord spotted one of the pirates in the crows nest with a spyglass and he was looking right in their direction.

"Oh no, I think he sees us. We are going to be captured!" shuddered Gord.

"Wait he is looking in our direction but not pointing or reacting in any way. I don't think that he can see us. We are invisible to them!" Adam said with excitement in his voice.

"You know Adam, I think you are right," said Gord with a sigh of relief.

"If they can't see us we can get closer and find out more.

Maybe we can finally unlock the mystery of the Phantom Ship," Molly suggested.

"Ha, ha, ha, ha," said Adam in his scariest voice.

"Shhhh, maybe they can hear us," whispered Molly.

"Let's find out," said Gord as he yelled at the top of his lungs, "Hey you dumb pirates, if you want to fight, bring it on!"

His voice echoed across the surface of the water. The three children waited while anticipating the worst, but nothing happened.

"They can't hear us either. This is great," said Adam. "We can row right out there and even get on their ship. What do you think guys, are you up for it?" he asked.

"Let's do it, let's go!" exclaimed Gord.

Molly, although hesitant, agreed with her brothers because really, what other choice was there? Slowly they rowed the boat towards the ship. It seemed like no time at all before they came along side of the pirate ship. They looked up and were almost frightened to death as there was a massive, scary, and ugly pirate throwing some soapy water over board. Molly covered her mouth to stifle a scream.

Gord, being the bravest of the three and being quite sure that they could not see or hear him, looked up and said, "Hey you dumb ugly pirate, why don't you get out of my face before I throw you overboard?"

Adam paused for a moment and laughed, then he added, "Wait a minute, when you were young, you were so ugly that your mother tied a pork chop around your neck so the dog would play with you."

They all laughed and Molly thought that she also would like to say something really nasty to the pirate but all she could think of was, "You are just plain ugly and I hate you for what you did to my Great Grandpa Ben," as a tear rolled down her cheek.

CHAPTER 30

All Aboard

Gord was first to grab the rope ladder that was hanging over the back of the ship.

"Come on you two, let's get to the bottom of this mystery," he suggested.

"Wait until I tie our boat to the bottom of the ladder. If we ever want to get back home we will need our boat," Adam replied.

The three children scrambled up the ladder onto the deck of the ship. They walked around totally undetected and felt as though they were secret spies.

"This is very weird," whispered Molly. "No one can see us or hear us. Watch this, boys," Molly continued as she made an ugly face right in front of a wobbling pirate.

The pirates were drinking a lot and celebrating their conquests in drunken merriment. Voices could be heard below deck in the captain pirate's cabin.

"Let's get closer and see what they are saying," said Gord. The children quietly snuck down the narrow stairs to the captain's cabin. The room was a little bit smaller than Aunt Ann's kitchen and there was a large table in the centre surrounded with big wooden chairs. A bar with lots of empty beer mugs lined one wall and several wooden kegs of rum stood in the corner. The captain and three other pirates were sitting around the table going through a small box of their treasures.

The captain was just a little man, very rugged looking with brown skin baked and dried by the sun. He had a nasty scar across the side of his face and he was complaining bitterly about the lack of valuable treasure taken that day. As he slammed his fist on the table four steins of rum shook and almost toppled over as all of the pirates grabbed their mugs. Then the children heard him say something that started a fire of hate inside their trembling bodies.

"What is this?" he said as he turned over the box onto the table. "A wedding ring, a locket with two hands holding a ruby, and an old photo of some lady! Is that all you found? What pray tell is this?" he yelled as he held up the wooden eye.

One of the pirates spoke up with an evil laugh in his voice. "That is the eye from that stupid fisherman whose boat we capsized. The picture is probably his beloved wife and that necklace, well that is a good luck charm for our conquest. Well, I guess his luck however, ran out today," he said with another hardy laugh as the others joined in.

"Ooooh, I'm so mad I could kill them!" Molly yelled. "Let's steal all that stuff back," she continued.

"No," said Adam, "remember, we have all that stuff back at the farm. We can't take anything or it will change the course of history, we must only observe."

CHAPTER 31

Molly Scares
the Pirates

Molly looked at Adam, and Gord, and then confirmed, "They can't see or hear us right?" The boys both nodded and watched Molly as she went over to the pirate who was bragging about capsizing her Great Grandpa's boat.

Each time he reached for his stein of rum, Molly moved it ever so slightly.

"I must be going crazy," said the pirate. "My mug seems to be moving."

The other pirates laughed at him and suggested that he should have another drink. Each time he reached for his drink Molly moved it just a little farther away. He looked at his mug and said, "I swear it is moving, look at it."

The other pirates looked and Molly did nothing. She

wanted them to think that he was crazy. This continued for a few minutes and finally when he wasn't looking she pushed the half full stein over, spilling it all over his lap. He cursed and swore and the others laughed at him calling him a clumsy donkey. All of the children had a good chuckle over this and thought about what they could do to get back at the terrible pirates who had sunk Ben's boat.

It was like a light bulb went on in Gord's head. "Watch this! I am going to scare the H – E – double hockey sticks out of these pirates!"

He walked over to the table and picked up the wooden eye while making an eerie, creepy sound. The pirates couldn't hear it but it added to the effect for Adam and Molly. Gord raised the eye as if it was floating and put it in front of the pirates. He moved it so it was looking at each of the pirates in turn. The big old pirate screamed and fell back in his chair, hitting his head on the floor. Gord followed him to the floor with the eye holding it in front of the pirates face. The pirate scrambled to his feet puffing and panting and ran up the narrow stairs screaming. Then, Gord steered the eye back to the three remaining pirates at the table and repeated the performance, all while saying in his scariest voice, "The evil eye is coming to get you!"

Soon the remaining pirates were sent screaming and scrambling up the narrow stairs, pushing each other over while trying to escape. Adam and Molly were laughing uncontrollably.

"That was so much fun," they both said together. Molly looked at the picture which accompanied 'Ruby's Hands'.

"Great Grandma Ruby was so pretty," she said as she looked longingly at the picture.

She remembered what Adam had said about not being

able to take anything because it would change the course of history. She knew that they already had the wooden eye and the pendant which she had lovingly named "Ruby's Hands", but they did not have this picture.

She thought, "What harm could a missing picture bring?" and she tucked it into the breast pocket of her overalls, unnoticed by the boys. She thought that this must be the missing picture from the family album.

The kids searched for a while longer through the cabin, to see if they could find anything else. After 15 minutes of opening drawers and cupboards, they came up empty handed.

"They obviously have a hiding place for their loot, like those caves," said Adam. "I think our mission is done here. Anyway we should be getting back before the adults get home, if they aren't already there worrying about us," he continued.

Gord agreed and said, "You head on down to the boat. There is just one more thing I have to do before we leave."

He pocketed the wooden eye and climbed up the rope ladder to the crow's nest where the lookout was. He pulled the eye out of his pocket and put it on the end of the spy glass. The lookout screamed and jumped back falling into the bay. He swam around to the ladder and climbed aboard the ship shivering from the cold, and trembling with fear.

"Now our mission is done here," Gord laughed as went back toward the cabin to replace the wooden eye back on the table.

"We still don't know why this ship is not burning or even if this is the right one," sighed Molly.

"Oh, this is the right one all right. Why else would they have all of Great Grampa Ben's stuff?" reasoned Adam.

The kids climbed down the rope ladder and got onto the

rowboat. As they started to row back to where the flaming keyhole was, they heard the pirates laughing, drinking and celebrating.

"Let's open another barrel of rum," they heard the captain say. Just then someone must have knocked the barrel of rum over and it spilled all over the deck when he was trying to open it.

The captain yelled, "You clumsy idiot, look at the mess you've made. You fools had better swab the deck."

CHAPTER 32

Sweet Revenge

A loud caw and a flutter of wings could be heard and out of the darkness of the sky, a huge crow started to circle the ship. It was as if he were looking for an opportunity to do something evil.

"That's Old Ben!" exclaimed Molly. The kids watched as Old Ben soared down and snatched a coal oil lantern in his beak, which was hanging on a nail. He soared back up into the sky, only to turn and drop it directly on the deck where the rum had spilled. The whole deck immediately exploded into flames and try as they did, the pirates were not able to extinguish the flames. Some pirates tried to climb up the masts to escape the flames which were engulfing the wooden ship like a wild fire tearing through a dry summer forest. Others jumped overboard to escape the heat. Now, the kids could feel the hot air from the flames as they rowed back further from the fiery ship. The men were screaming and crying as the flames followed them up the masts, setting their clothes ablaze. They cried out those recognizable screams that the children had heard on previous occasions, but these were much louder and definitely more terrifying. One by one the pirates fell into the depths of the water, some of them dead before they hit, while others hit the surface only to sink into the darkness of the bay.

This time, there were lots of fizzling sounds as the burning pirates fell overboard. Moments later Gord, Adam, and Molly witnessed the charred remains of the once majestic pirate ship, as it sank beneath the surface of the bay. The kids were awe struck and did not speak for a few minutes.

"Wow, Old Ben sure got even with those pirates for capsizing his boat," whispered Molly. "Do you think they deserved that?" she continued sadly.

"Now we know what happened to those pirates, but I guess the mystery of why the ghosts return to haunt the townspeople Shigawake, will remain unknown," reported Adam in his best announcer's voice.

CHAPTER 33

Was it All a Dream?

The children were rowing back to where the flaming keyhole was but as they passed the spot where they were sure it was, the keyhole did not appear. It seemed that for the briefest of moments, time stood still. No one said or did anything; no one dared to move or to speak. This silence was accompanied by everything becoming dark and very silent.

The next thing that happened was unexplainable. All three kids were asleep on the beach by the cave where they had been waiting to watch for signs of the Phantom Ship rising from the water. Adam stretched and yawned.

"We must have fallen asleep. Wow what a strange dream I had. We went back in time and were invisible and we were on the pirate's ship and Old Ben dropped a lantern and set the ship afire," said Adam.

"Wow, I had a very similar dream," said Gord. "The pirates were afraid, they weren't so tough," he continued.

"I didn't dream at all" said Molly, as she put her hand into the breast pocket of her overhauls and felt the picture of Ruby that she had taken from the pirate ship. Finally the album would be complete.

The End

Author Biography:

Al Eden is a retired middle school teacher who still substitutes 3-4 days a week. On the other days, he enjoys hanging out with his six year old grandson, fixing up the house, reading, and writing. Al enjoys being outdoors and he especially likes camping and vacationing to warm destinations with his wife. This is where he does most of his writing and creative thinking.

He has always enjoyed sports, and played college basketball while growing up. He took his love of sports and story-telling and relayed this to his four children and six grandchildren, who are all avid readers and sports enthusiasts. Al enjoys reading books to all ages, and has developed a passion for writing stories. Although he is a first time author, he has nearly finished the sequel to The Mystery of the Phantom Ship.

CPSIA information can be obtained
at www.ICGtesting.com
Printed in the USA
LVHW092140210220
647701LV00001B/9